"I'm at a point in my life that I need to make some decisions... It's time I made some kind of a life for myself, somewhere, somehow," Nathan said.

Violet nodded. "I know what you mean."

He chuckled. "I'm not even sure I know what I mean. I don't even know why you've been so nice to me. A woman like you should be friends with a solid, dependable man who knows where life is going to take him—knows what he wants."

"You'll figure it out."

He pressed his lips together and nodded.

"I'll miss you."

"Will you?" He smiled at her.

"Very much." She had to let him know she liked him without saying it in so many words.

"I might be back. I will make some decisions soon. Bye, Violet."

"Bye, Nathan."

He turned to leave and she watched him walk away. She wondered if that was the man she was going to marry.

That was certainly what she hoped, and what she prayed for.

Samantha Price is a bestselling author who knew she wanted to become a writer at the age of seven, after her grandmother read her *The Tale of Peter Rabbit*. Though the adventures of Peter started Samantha on her creative journey, it is now her love of Amish culture that inspires her. Her writing is wholesome with more than a dash of sweetness. Samantha lives in a quaint Victorian cottage with three rambunctious dogs.

AMISH VIOLET

Samantha Price

ISBN-13: 978-1-335-45490-4

Amish Violet

This edition published by arrangement with Harlequin Books S.A.

For questions and comments about the quality of this book, please contact us at CustomerService@Harlequin.com.

Printed in U.S.A.

Chapter One

Nancy stared at her sister, Nerida, wondering how she could bring up the subject. It had been some years since the last of Nancy's four daughters had gotten married and it was high time there was another wedding in the family. In short, it was her niece Violet's turn to get married. The trouble was, Violet was an introvert who preferred her own company to that of those around her. The next sentence that came out of her sister's mouth pleased Nancy enormously.

"Do you remember a few years ago, just after Lily got married, that you offered your help in finding a man for Violet?"

Nancy remembered it was Nerida who asked her. She never actually offered her help, but that didn't matter so much. *"Jah.* Has that been on your mind all this time?"

Nerida chortled. "Only over the last few days. We've both been so busy with other things, but now Violet is well over eighteen."

"You want my help now?"

"Jah, John and I have been worried about her. You know she's not… Well, she's a quiet girl. Will you help

us? Each of your girls has married a lovely man and I want the same for Violet."

Nancy's face beamed. "I'd love to help."

Nerida shook her head and looked down at the kitchen table where they both sat. "She worries me because she's so quiet, and she's barely been out of the *haus* since she's had to start wearing those glasses."

"That's exactly why she needs our help, Nerida."

"Do you think so?"

"I know so. She needs more confidence as well as the right man. If she has no confidence, she won't act appropriately when the right man comes along."

"I guess you're right."

"I usually am."

"Well…"

Nancy cackled. "Don't you start."

Nerida laughed and then pushed her chair out and stood up. "More tea?"

Nancy stared at the contents of the plain white china teacup. She drained the last mouthful. *"Jah, denke."* She placed the teacup down onto her saucer and Nerida picked up the pot and poured her some fresh tea. "Now sit down and don't try to change the subject."

"I won't. I admit I need your help. And I'm ready to get started on whatever you plan that we should do." Nerida sat again and looked directly at her older sister.

"Why are you bringing this up now, Nerida? Is there a young man you've found who you think might suit her?"

"Nee."

Nancy said, "Just because I haven't said anything doesn't mean I haven't been thinking about your girls and what will become of them." Nancy looked away from her sister. She'd probably said too much.

Nerida narrowed her eyes. "What do you mean by that, Nancy?"

"I mean everybody needs help. Well, not everybody, but if *Gott* hasn't chosen to place someone in her way before now, she plainly needs our help."

Nerida sighed as she slumped further into her chair. "Maybe you're right."

Relief washed over Nancy. She'd saved herself from an awkward situation and she even had Nerida agreeing with her.

"What shall we do, Nancy?"

"The first thing we need to do is make a list of all the young men in the community that would suit her—all of them."

Nerida drummed her fingers on the wooden kitchen table. "Should we find out which ones she likes first?"

Nancy threw her head back and laughed. "Girls her age don't know what time of day it is, let alone what kind of husband would be good for them."

"I don't know if that's true. When I was her age, John and I were married already."

"Well, things are different in these modern times."

They both looked around when they heard someone walk into the kitchen. It was Willow.

"Hello, Aunt Nancy." Willow hurried toward Nancy and hugged her tightly and Nancy gave her a pat on the back.

When Willow straightened, Nancy asked, "How's my favorite niece doing today?"

Willow giggled at her aunt. Nancy always called each of her nieces her "favorite niece." "I'm good."

"Why don't you run along, Willow? Aunt Nancy and I are having a private discussion."

Willow's eyes opened wide. "What about?"

"Not about you, if that's what you're worried about." Nancy gave a laugh.

Willow's head whipped around and she stared at her mother. "About Violet?"

Nerida answered, "We're just having a private discussion; it doesn't have to be about anyone."

"It normally is," Willow said, now standing with her hands on her hips.

"Go and check the washing on the line, see if it's dry, and then see what food we're running low on for the livestock."

"*Dat* keeps an eye on the animal food."

"Willow, what have I told you about doing what you're told when you're told?"

"I'm going." Willow sighed and walked away, dragging her feet.

Nerida called after her, "After you've finished doing that, why don't you go find your *schweschder?* I think she's paying her respects to Lorraine's friends. She went to Molly Gingerich's."

"*Jah,* okay. I'll do that after I check on the washing."

Once Willow was out of the room, Nerida leaned forward. "Now, where were we?"

"We were talking about making a list of all the eligible bachelors. And if there are none who are suitable, we'll have to broaden our search and look further afield."

"Surely there'll be someone who's right for her here in this community. I don't want her moving away." Nerida's mouth downturned.

"We'll just have to hope and pray that someone from around these parts will suit her."

"I suppose we should be thinking about Lorraine's funeral rather than being selfish and thinking about our own family," Nerida said.

"Valerie and I have got all that under control. Valerie's doing most of the organizing since Lorraine's son is useless for that."

"It wonders me why he's come back here after all this time."

"Well, he'd have to go to his *mudder's* funeral and now he'll probably live in the *haus* since he's probably got nowhere else to live."

"That's a bit harsh, Nancy. I've never heard you speak that way."

Nancy lifted her chin. "He wasn't around when she was sick. If he was, I didn't see him. I'm sorry, but he's got no care or thought for anyone but himself." She nodded her head sharply. "That's what it seems like to me."

Chapter Two

As Violet saw Mrs. Gingerich's small house, a wave of sorrow washed over her, knowing the old woman had lost her good friend.

Lorraine Beiler had been a lovely woman who had brought joy to everyone around her before she'd gotten ill. Violet had known her all her life, and the last two years, she'd slipped down in health. It was shortly after Lorraine's husband had died that she'd gotten sick, and Violet was certain that she'd died of a broken heart.

Violet's mother was always one to rally around the grieving family members at times like these. Violet often accompanied her mother on these trips, but Molly Gingerich and her mother hadn't always gotten along. That's why Violet had come on her own.

When Violet tried to open the front gate, she saw it was tied up with a rope. Unable to see a way to undo it, she picked up the lower edge of her dress and climbed over the top, hoping no one would see the unladylike antic. It seemed that the old lady might have been trying to discourage visitors.

A few minutes later, after several knocks, the door

slowly opened and Mrs. Gingerich stood there staring up at her. At first, the woman didn't speak or even smile. She looked past Violet and then up and down the street.

"Are you here alone?" she asked, opening the door slightly wider.

"Jah, I came alone."

She pushed the door open fully. "Come in."

Violet stepped inside, waited, and then followed her as she walked into the kitchen.

She pointed to the table. "Sit down."

After Violet did what she'd been told, Mrs. Gingerich sat next to her, and said, "What's a young girl like you coming to see me for?"

"I came to see how you are. I know Lorraine was a good friend of yours, and I know you must be missing her. That's why I stopped by."

"Denke for coming." The old woman slowly smiled and peered into her face. "Can I get you anything? I've just made some ginger beer."

"I'd like that very much, *denke."* The old lady was a good twenty to thirty years older than Lorraine, since Lorraine had to have been in her fifties and Mrs. Gingerich must've been in her seventies.

Mrs. Gingerich placed a glass of ginger beer in front of Violet. After she took a sip and complimented the old woman on the taste, she asked, "Do you know what ever happened to Lorraine's son?"

"Jah, I do. Nathan's back."

Violet's eyes opened wide. "Is he?" Violet had grown up with Nathan Beiler, gone through school at the same time, and they'd always gotten along. In truth, she'd had a crush on him for years. He'd left the community shortly after his father had died.

"Jah, he's living back where he was."

"In Lorraine's *haus?"*

"Jah."

"He must feel dreadful. His *vadder* died two years ago and now his *mudder* has gone. He's so young and he's got no one."

"It's no use him being back now. He should've been back here when she was sick and needed caring for. Although, from time to time I did see a car parked out front of Lorraine's *haus.* Maybe he did visit." The old lady shook her head.

"Is he back to stay?"

She shook her head again. "I don't know. I haven't heard. Cookies? Would you like some sugar cookies? I only baked them recently."

"Okay. Lovely, *denke."*

Mrs. Gingerich rustled around in her cupboard and then placed a tin of cookies on the table in front of Violet. As Violet reached out to take one, the old woman asked, "Where's your *mudder* today?"

"She's at home. Aunt Nancy came to visit and they're at home talking."

"Did *she* send you here?"

"Who, Nancy or *Mamm?"*

"Either one."

"Nee. I came here on my own because I know you're a good friend...um, you were a good friend of Lorraine's."

"Denke. We weren't that close."

"Oh, I thought you were."

"Nee. You're a nice girl. Just make sure you stay that way. It can't be easy for you."

Violet resisted asking why or what couldn't be easy

for her and munched on a cookie instead. She guessed it had something to do with what Mrs. Gingerich thought of her mother.

"Did you know your *mudder* and I used to get along once?"

"Nee, I didn't know that."

"She's not easy to get along with, you know. Well, *jah,* I suppose you do know that."

Violet raised her eyebrows and remained silent. It was most likely true, since *Mamm* had been in a long disagreement with her own sister. It had lasted most of Violet's life. Only in the last couple of years had they started being close once again, and Aunt Nancy still seemed cautious about whatever she said. "Did you have a falling out over something in particular?" Violet asked.

Mrs. Gingerich laughed. "It was years ago. We had an argument over cake. I barely remember the whole thing now. I was aggravated how your *mudder* thinks she can do everything better than anybody else."

"Oh, I didn't know."

"Nee. You wouldn't. You must take after your *vadder.* Your *mudder* is very competitive. I think it's to do with her living under Nancy's shadow as her younger *schweschder."*

"Er...*jah.* One or two people have mentioned she's competitive."

"Now, your Aunt Nancy is a different one. She's always helping others. She's always looking after the sick, taking them soup, and visiting them."

"She's very kind. My *mudder* does a lot of things like that too, though. She's always out and about seeing where she can be of service."

"Your *mudder* could learn a thing or two from her older *schweschder.*"

"She's been a *gut mudder* to me," Violet said in her mother's defense.

"You'd have to say that."

"I mean it. It's true. I know she gets on the wrong side of a lot of people and I don't know why. She doesn't mean to. Anyway, I didn't come here to talk about my *mudder.* I came to see how you are."

"I'll miss Lorraine. I couldn't see her as much as I would've liked due to my failing health."

"Jah, she'll be missed. She was a nice lady."

After another hour and another glass of ginger beer, Violet said goodbye to Mrs. Gingerich and started off back home. It was an hour's walk back to her house, and Violet loved to walk in the sun in the springtime. The sun warmed her skin as she made her way down the tree-lined road while the sunlight dappled its way through the trees.

In the distance, she caught sight of Willow running toward her. Fearing something was wrong because she'd not seen Willow run since she was a child, she ran to meet her.

"Willow, what is it?"

Willow doubled over, trying to catch her breath. When she straightened, she was still huffing and puffing and her full cheeks were bright red.

"Is *Mamm* okay?" Violet asked, fearing the worst. Then she thought of her father. "Is *Dat* okay?"

"Jah, and *jah,"* Willow managed to say in between sharp breaths.

"Well, what is it?"

"They were talking about you."

The only "they" Willow could've been talking about was her mother and Aunt Nancy. "*Mamm* and Aunt Nancy?"

Willow put her hands on her hips and nodded.

"What did they say?"

"They're getting you married off."

Violet didn't like the sound of that. Marry her off to who? "And you ran all that way just to tell me?"

"*Jah.* I thought you'd want to know."

Violet forced a giggle, not wanting her sister to see she was concerned.

"It's not funny, Violet."

Still laughing, Violet said, "There was no need to upset yourself and run all this way. They're always talking about silly stuff like that."

Willow looked a little upset at her giggles. "They were making a plan and writing a list."

That didn't sound good. Violet could no longer put on an act. "What? A list for what?"

"A list of bachelors."

Violet tugged on the strings of her prayer *kapp*. It sounded serious if they were making a list. "*Denke* for telling me, Willow."

"What are you going to do?"

"I'll tell them I'm not interested."

"*Nee,* you can't say anything. Then they'll know I was listening in and I'll get into trouble again. You can't."

"What do you suggest I do?"

"They can't force you to get married."

"*Nee,* but they can make my life awfully uncomfortable in the process of trying. And what about the poor men they've picked for me? None of them will be interested either." Violet rolled her eyes.

"You can't say you weren't warned that they'd do this."

"I know. Both Lily and Daisy told me what they were like, but I thought I might've escaped it. I was sure Aunt Nancy would consider me a lost cause. All the cousins are so pretty and I'm not. I'm plain. I'm a plain Jane."

"Because of your glasses?"

"Nee, but *denke* for reminding me about that."

"You still look pretty."

"You don't have to try to make me feel better. I know what I look like."

Willow's eyebrows flew upward. "I think you're pretty, I do."

Violet pulled a face. "Yeah, well, what *you* think doesn't count."

"It counts for me."

Violet laughed. *"Denke,* but you know what I mean."

"You want to get married some day though, right?"

"Some day, but only to someone special. I won't marry just anyone as though I'm desperate."

"The bishop's *fraa* says it doesn't matter who you marry. She says as long as you're both in the community, it'll work out."

"That's okay for her to say because she's already made her choice. I'm not marrying someone totally disagreeable just to be married. There is no way I'd do that."

"That's what I thought you'd say. That's why I ran all the way to tell you. *Mamm* said you'd be at old Molly's house."

"*Denke,* and now that you're here you can come with me while I'm visiting."

"Who are you off to see now?"

"I'm off to see Lorraine's son, Nathan."

"What? *Nee,* Violet, I'm not going with you to see him, and no one else would want to. He's a backslider and hasn't been to a meeting in two years or more. Don't worry about him."

"Stop it, Willow. He's a friend. We used to go to *schul* with him."

"He's not my friend. You know what *Dat* says about us being around people like him."

Violet shook her head at her younger sister. She had such a different attitude to things than Violet did.

Chapter Three

Violet was taken aback by her sister's response. This wasn't about who was, or who wasn't, a member of the community. The young man's mother had died. Surely everyone needed comfort at a time like this. Besides, he hadn't been shunned and there was nothing to prevent her from stopping by to see him.

"Willow," she said, and then paused, thinking how best to express her disappointment in her attitude. "He's a human being and he would be grieving more than anyone else in the community. His *mudder* just died, and as far as I know he has no one to help him through this time."

Willow stood, saying nothing. It was clear to Violet that Willow wanted nothing to do with Nathan Beiler. Her silence was evidence of Willow not wishing to enter into a disagreement with her.

"I'm going there right now. You can either come or stay, but I'm going. He's staying at his *mudder's haus* and he's most likely staying there by himself." Violet knew that last bit would make Willow feel obliged to go with her to save her from the possible scandal of visiting the young man alone.

Willow looked down at the ground and shuffled her black boots around in the dirt. “All right, I’ll go with you, but I’ll not say one word to him, not one word.”

As Violet and Willow set off arm-in-arm, Violet tried to understand the unwillingness in Willow to visit Nathan.

No one knew why he had stopped going to the meetings, and the young people’s outings, too. He’d cut all contact with the community and its members. It was said that his mother had tried to convince him to return, but he’d refused.

A few minutes later, they entered the yard of the Beiler house. It looked all closed up; the windows were shut and the curtains were drawn.

“Seems there’s no one at home,” Willow said, turning to leave.

Violet ignored her and continued up the porch steps toward the front door. She knocked, waited, and then knocked again. A few moments later, the door opened.

Nathan had opened the main wooden door, but he left the screen-door locked between them. Violet got the unspoken message that he wasn’t interested in speaking to either of them.

“Can I help you?” he asked.

It was hard to see him through the screen. “Is that you, Nathan?”

“Yes.” He unlocked the door and flung it open. “Yeah, it’s me. Hi, Violet.” He looked over at Willow and then back to Violet.

This was not the boy she’d remembered; Nathan Beiler was now a man and, surprisingly, he was a handsome one—gone was the tall gangly boy she remembered. His shoulders were wide and his build was solid; his eyes were the same soft brown she remembered, accentuated by thick dark eyebrows and lashes.

Violet realized that Willow truly intended to remain silent, and that meant that she'd have to be the one to do the talking. Violet cleared her throat. "Hello, Nathan. We've just come to offer our condolences and to let you know that your *mudder* will be missed."

He looked again at each of them in turn, before he let out a heavy sigh and lowered his head. "Thank you. I'm sure my mother would've appreciated you both coming by."

His voice had a slightly different tone to it and possibly that might have been because he wasn't speaking in Pennsylvania Dutch.

"We would love to sit down with you. Is that possible?" Violet glanced behind her at Willow and was annoyed that she was still silent and standing so rigidly. Even though Willow had not wanted to come, Violet thought she was making her dislike of Nathan far too obvious.

"I'm sorry. I'm kind of in the middle of something," Nathan said.

"Okay, I understand. Let me know if we can help with anything. I think that Valerie is looking after some aspects of the funeral."

"Yes. Valerie's been a great help." He nodded.

"Please don't hesitate to contact me if you need help with anything."

"Thank you."

"Do you remember where we live?"

"Sure. I haven't forgotten where you live, Violet."

She gave an embarrassed giggle. "I thought you might have forgotten." Since it was a small community and everyone knew where everyone else lived, of course he would remember.

"Thanks for stopping by," he said, a little too pointedly.

They said their goodbyes and then the girls left.

When they were far enough away so Nathan wouldn't hear, Violet glanced back at the house before she reprimanded her sister. "You could've hidden your disapproval a little better. You know he noticed, don't you?"

Willow shrugged off Violet's harsh words. "It was obvious that he didn't want us there. You dragged me there knowing I didn't want to go. I had no reason to pretend that I wanted to be there."

"Willow, he's just lost his *mudder.* People do things that they wouldn't normally do when they are experiencing great pain. It is our job to help him; we're doing *Gott's* work."

"He isn't like this because she died; he's always been like it. He always stayed by himself and didn't socialize with anyone. He thinks he's better than us."

Violet stopped in her tracks. "He's not been shunned, Willow. He never got baptized. He's still welcome at the meetings and at the gatherings. I don't know why you're being so mean."

Willow stormed off ahead, her long brown dress swishing along the roadside with every step while Violet followed some distance behind her. Glad to be alone, Violet took the chance to sort through her thoughts.

She wondered how she would have felt if her last living family member died, especially her beloved mother.

She knew, without a doubt, that it would be tough; she felt the pain and loneliness that Nathan must've felt.

While Willow had taken the right-hand fork in the road and was now a miniature figure in the distance, Violet kept to the left where she would run into Valerie's house. Valerie was an old family friend and had become her confidant.

As she approached Valerie's house, Violet saw her outside, saying goodbye to a visitor who was leaving in a buggy. It was Ed Bontrager. She knew it was him from his black horse who had one white sock on his right front leg. Ed was a widower and Valerie was a widow. They spent a great deal of time together, and Violet was certain that anytime now they'd announce their wedding even though neither one of them had ever admitted to any kind of relationship with the other. Violet had heard a whisper from her Aunt Nancy that Valerie and Ed had been sweet on each other before they'd each married different people. Violet had never asked Valerie any questions and neither had Valerie offered any information about why she and Ed hadn't married each other way back then.

She walked on toward the house and when the buggy passed, Ed smiled and gave her a wave. She waved back and kept walking up the driveway to Valerie, who was waiting for her outside her house.

"Hello, Violet. It's a nice day for a walk."

"It is, but I'm through with walking. I've done far too much today. Much more than I thought I was going to do when I started out." Violet gave a little giggle, trying to distract herself from her aching leg muscles which were sending off little pings. They always did that when she walked a great distance.

"Come in and I'll fix you some meadow tea."

"Denke." As soon as she walked into the house, she inhaled the aroma of something that was cooking. "Have you been baking?"

"I've been making some things for Lorraine's funeral—cookies and such."

"Is everyone coming back here after it?"

"I was going to talk to Nathan about that. I stopped by to see him this morning and he wasn't there."

"I saw him just now."

"Where was he?"

"At the *haus.* I went there just now with Willow."

"How was he?"

"He was okay, I think. I don't know, really. He's probably depressed. It must be awful for him with his *vadder* gone and now his *mudder.* He didn't invite us in, but I guess I wouldn't feel like having guests to the *haus* if one of my parents had just died."

"The funeral is the day after tomorrow. I'll go see him later today. I'm certain he won't mind me having the people come back here after the funeral. He's a man after all, and he probably doesn't know the first thing about feeding a crowd."

"I think you're probably right. He said you'd been a good help. His *haus* looked all closed up. He must've been sitting inside in the darkness and with no fresh air."

"I wonder if he was home when I went there earlier. He could've been asleep, come to think of it. I knocked loud enough, but if he was a sound sleeper he could've slept through it. He gave the funeral director instructions. He didn't want to have a viewing at his home."

"Oh. Is there going to be a viewing at all?"

"Jah. The bishop's having it at his place."

"I see." Violet nodded.

Valerie poured out a glass of iced meadow tea for Violet and one for herself before she joined Violet at the table.

"Cheer an old woman up, Violet. You must have something to tell me that'll brighten my day."

Violet gave a little giggle. Valerie had just had Ed there. Hadn't he brightened up her day? Maybe the rumors about them weren't correct. "Did you know that *Mamm* and Aunt Nancy are plotting to get me married off?"

"Nee, but it doesn't surprise me. Who are they planning to marry you to? Do they have a man in mind?"

While running her finger around the rim of the glass, she said, "That's something I don't know. Willow overheard them this morning talking about it. They're going to write out a list."

Valerie laughed. "That cheers me up. I'm glad you told me."

"It might sound funny, but what if they put pressure on me? That'll make my life miserable."

"I can understand that. Do you want me to talk to them?" Valerie asked.

Violet gasped. *"Nee.* They don't know that Willow heard. She's already been in trouble for eavesdropping before. I'm not too worried about it."

"Jah, gut. I wouldn't worry about it either. Just stand your ground. Tell them how you feel. It'll happen when it happens. You'll find love when it's meant to happen."

"Okay, I will stand up to them."

Valerie laughed. "That's the way. Do you want to come with me to see Nathan this afternoon?"

Violet shook her head. *"Nee, denke.* I've already seen him once today. He might think I like him if I go back there again." Violet sipped on the sweet, minty, cold meadow tea. "I'd like to help you where I can with the funeral and everything, though."

"I'd appreciate your help. You can certainly help me on the day. I'll be able to find plenty to keep you busy."

"I'd like that. Keeping busy away from *Mamm* and Aunt Nancy. They're probably scheming that there will be a lot of outside visitors coming to the funeral."

"Possibly," Valerie agreed.

That night, Violet knelt by her bed and said a small prayer for Nathan, before she climbed in between the sheets covered by her warm quilt. She could not help but wonder why Nathan had chosen not to attend the gatherings or the singings. All young people in the community loved the singings. Neither had he attended any volleyball days or ice-skating in the last two winter seasons. She was certain no one else in the community besides Valerie was making an effort toward him.

The next day was the day before Lorraine's funeral and Violet decided to write Nathan a letter. From her letter, she wanted him to know that he was not alone and that someone was there for him. She was taught to help others, and that is just what she planned to do. When she finished the short letter, she decided to put it under his door and hurry away. She didn't like the idea of more walking and when she was nearly halfway to his house, she saw young Toby Yoder.

"Hey, Toby."

He was no relation to Hezekiah Yoder, her uncle. There were many Yoders in their community.

Toby saw her and ran over. *"Jah,* Violet."

"Would you do something for me?"

"Jah, anything."

"Would you take this letter to Nathan Beiler's *haus* and see to it that he gets it personally?"

"I sure will."

"Denke." She was just about to hand it over when she pulled the letter back toward her. "And no peeking."

The boy smiled. "I get the picture."

"I will bake some cookies and bring them to the next Sunday meeting."

"No need to do that. I like doing things for people."

"And I like baking cookies for people."

The boy laughed. "Okay, *denke.* I do like cookies."

"I thought you might." Violet handed the letter over and the boy took off running.

"Denke, Toby."

He didn't answer and Violet watched him run, wondering where he got all the energy from. She was glad she didn't have to walk that extra distance and back again.

Chapter Four

"*Gott,* please give me the strength and courage to get through this, Amen." Nathan prayed as he did every morning.

He was grateful that Valerie and Violet had both visited him the previous day and he could feel God was showing him that there were people in the community who cared about him.

He held his Bible in his hands and sat down on his bed. Looking around the room in the house that was now solely his, he could find little reason to rejoice. Prayer normally made him feel better, but nothing made him feel happy since the death of his mother. He hadn't appreciated her enough when she was alive and now he had no one. Even though he was a grown man, he felt like an orphaned child with no roots to anything or anyone. He'd miss her on his daily visits to her and he didn't know how he hadn't noticed she'd been so ill.

When his father had lost his way some years back and had fallen into drunkenness, the community abandoned him and he'd been shunned. That meant Nathan and his mother could no longer eat their food at the same table as *Dat.* That did nothing to stop his father's drinking and only created more tension in the household.

As far as Nathan was concerned, the people in the community were only supportive when it pleased them, and in his eyes, that did not represent what a Christian should be. To them, his father had sinned, and that made him less than worthy to be one of them. It was for that reason that Nathan decided that he could no longer be a member of the Amish community. He preferred to worship alone, in his own way. *Let he who is without sin cast the first stone,* he often thought, *as there is no one who is perfect.*

He could see from the way that Violet had looked at him that she'd pitied him and he didn't want pity. He wanted Violet to see him in a far different light. As for her sister, Willow, she could barely look at him and he wondered if that was what was in store for him at his mother's funeral. Would they all be staring at him, looking, and judging?

They all thought he was the lost sheep and he allowed them to think it. The possibility that they could be at fault was absurd to them, so it must have been him. Nathan had told his mother he'd not left God, he'd only left the community, but she couldn't understand and thought they were one and the same thing.

Still, he had to admit that it was good of the bishop to offer his home for the viewing before the funeral, and Valerie to offer the use of hers afterward.

He replaced his Bible and stood up when he heard a knock on his front door. It was a boy he knew from the community, one of the Yoder boys, and he'd grown taller. Nathan was both confused and surprised. Visits from people in the community were out of the ordinary, but perhaps to be expected until after his mother's funeral was over.

"Can I help you?" Nathan asked.

The boy handed him a letter. "Violet asked me to give this to you."

Cautiously taking the letter, Nathan thanked the boy and he turned and walked away.

She was just here; why would she write? Curiosity got the best of him as he quickly opened the letter.

Dear Nathan,

I know that you are going through the most difficult time of your life, but I want you to know that God will help you through this if you allow Him. He said, "Never will I leave you; Never will I forsake you." He can give you the comfort you need through this and help you to heal.

You haven't been to the meetings in a long time, but I'm encouraging you to come. We're your family and can help you in any way you need. We are here for you.

I'm going to be helping Valerie with some of the arrangements, so I'll be speaking to you soon.

Your friend,

Violet

Nathan held the letter in his hand and sat down on the couch. His heart softened at the kindness he felt coming through the written words on the page.

She was a nice girl, and as he gave more thought to her offer to help, he realized it might be a good idea to accept. He'd told Valerie that he wanted to be involved in the funeral arrangements, but didn't know the first thing to do. The sensible thing was to write back to her, so he jumped up and hurried to the door. When he saw the boy still by the front gate, he called out to him.

"Hey."

The boy turned around. *"Jah?"*

"Can you take a note back to Violet? I'll pay you."

"Yeah, okay."

The boy made his way back and Nathan left the door wide open for him while he looked for pen and paper. "I won't be a minute. I'll just jot something down. What's your name again?"

"It's Toby Yoder."

"Thanks for doing this, Toby."

"You're welcome. *Denke* for the money."

"Do you remember me?"

"Nathan Beiler. Your *mudder* just died."

"That's right."

"I can do odd jobs around here too if you want."

Nathan looked at the boy, surprised by his offer. "I'll keep that in mind, but I don't think I'll be around for long." He took hold of the pen. *Dear Violet? No, it sounds too formal. Just Violet would be better.*

Violet,

Thank you for reaching out to me. It is rather unusual from members of the community, and I really do appreciate it.

This period is indeed difficult, but I'm learning more and more each day to take comfort from God and to allow Him to help me. He has guided me and is still guiding me through this. I know, one day, this will get easier.

I appreciate everything Valerie has done, but

it's my place to make decisions regarding my mother and I will take over, or assist, Valerie with it.
Thank you for being kind, Violet.
Nathan

He folded the letter and handed it to Toby. "Hang on." After he found his wallet he gave the boy five dollars.

"*Denke,* Nathan. Wow!" The boy rushed out with the note clutched in his hand.

Nathan laughed and when the boy was gone, he closed the door. Whether it was because he was touched by Violet's offer of help, Nathan wasn't sure, but he felt deep down in his heart that things might not be as bleak as they'd seemed. That message from Violet had lifted his spirits and was just what he needed.

Nerida was standing by her kitchen window, scrubbing the kitchen sink, when she saw young Toby Yoder running toward the house. He wasn't one of the usual children she saw playing in the area and he appeared to be heading directly to her house. She tossed the cleaning rag in the sink, wiped off her hands on a towel, and hurried to see what he wanted. Stepping down the porch chairs, she waved to him. "Hello, Toby."

"Hello, Ma'am."

"What brings you so far from your place?"

"I'm running an errand." His cheeks were rosy under his freckles, and he was slightly out of breath.

"Have you been running?"

"*Jah*. I like running. I can run for miles."

Noticing something clutched in his hand, she looked down and saw a folded piece of paper. "Is that a note?"

"Jah, I'm to give it to Violet and no one else."

"And can I ask who the sender of this note might be?"

The young boy looked thoughtful. "I don't know if I'm supposed to say."

"Violet's my *dochder."*

"Jah, I know, but I reckon I'm supposed to hand it to her."

"You wait in the kitchen for milk and cookies, and I'll take the note up to Violet. She's in her bedroom."

He smiled. *"Denke.* Chocolate cookies?"

"Jah. I have both chocolate and chocolate chip."

"Chocolate chip are my favorite."

"Then that's what you shall have."

He handed the note over and with her arm around his shoulder, she walked him up the porch steps. When they stepped inside, Nerida said, "The kitchen is that way. You wait there and I'll be back in a minute."

The boy nodded and headed to the kitchen.

Nerida looked down at the piece of paper in her hands. Who was Violet getting secret notes from? It could only be from someone of whom she did not approve. There was only one likely candidate who was showing Violet attention and that was Nathan Beiler.

She held the note up to the light and couldn't see any writing. Would it be wrong to take a peek inside? The worst thing imaginable would be if Violet ran away with an *Englischer* and if peeking in the letter would save that happening, what would be wrong with that?

With her heart pounding, she glanced around to make sure no one was looking, then she took hold of one corner and then carefully peeled it back.

"May I get myself a glass of water?"

Nerida looked across at Toby. *"Jah,* of course."

"That note's for Violet's eyes only, Ma'am."

"Ach jah, I know. I was just…making sure it was for Violet."

Toby's expression didn't change and neither did his tone. "It is."

"I'll get your milk and cookies in a minute. Go back and wait in the kitchen."

"Jah, Ma'am."

It was an impossible situation and guilt washed over Nerida. What a bad example it would've been if Toby had seen her spying on her daughter by reading her private letter.

Seeing Toby was now back in the kitchen, she knew she'd have to trust Violet and leave everything in God's hands.

When Willow came down the stairs, Nerida said, "Willow, Toby Yoder's in the kitchen. I said I'd get him cookies and milk; can you see to that?"

"What's he doing here?"

"I'll tell you later. Just do as I said."

"Okay."

Chapter Five

Violet anxiously awaited a response from Nathan. It would be stupid of her to think that he had to answer. She paced her bedroom floor while rubbing her palms together. She did not understand why she was so anxious, but she felt a sense of responsibility toward him.

Her *mudder* called out to her. She rushed downstairs. *"Jah, Mamm?"*

"Someone left this for you." She handed her the letter and narrowed her eyes. "Who's it from?"

She stared at the letter, delighted that he'd written her a note and gotten it to her so quickly. "Nathan Beiler, I'd expect." Violet felt disapproval emanating from her mother.

"What's the matter, *Mamm?"* Violet asked, staring at the look of horror on her mother's face.

Through a clenched jaw, her mother said, "I don't want you speaking to that boy."

"Why not?"

"Because he's troubled; the devil is in that boy."

"Mamm, the devil isn't in him. I'm worried about

him, that's all. Since his *mudder* died, he's got no one. I offered to help with the funeral tomorrow."

Her *mudder* lifted up her chin. "As soon as it's done, I want you far away from him. He had young Toby Yoder deliver that note and I think it's a bad example for him to see notes being passed around in secret."

"Where's Toby?"

"In the kitchen. Willow's getting him milk and cookies."

Violet nodded and left the room, dragging her feet. Once back in her room, she read the letter and couldn't help smiling. She would've felt silly and embarrassed if he hadn't responded. Rather than sending another letter back, she'd slip out of the house and go and see him so they could speak face-to-face. Looking again at the letter, she admired his handwriting. It was strong, confident, and elegant at the same time. She had never noticed anyone's handwriting before, but she found his writing to be attractive.

When Toby had left, Violet was waiting for Willow when she came back upstairs.

"Cover for me, Willow. You'll have to help *Mamm* with the dinner and other chores. I'm going back to see Nathan."

Lines appeared in Willow's young forehead as her eyebrows shot up. "What do you mean?"

"He wrote a note to me because I wrote one to him. Anyway, I'm going to hitch the buggy and go see him."

Willow's bottom jaw dropped. "What if they find out?"

"Will you cover for me?"

Willow grunted. "I'll try. Don't be long."

"Denke. I won't."

Violet hurried out of the house. There was no way she wanted to do more walking so she hitched the spare buggy and was careful to do so on the other side of the barn, out of sight. Her mother usually watched everything that was going on outside the kitchen window.

Violet's stomach gnawed away at her. Was it hunger, or was she nervous? She wasn't certain which it was.

All the way to Nathan's house, she thought about him. Nathan certainly did not look like he had the devil in him. He looked like a regular man, even handsome. More than anything, she hoped he would let her in the house this time, or she would be embarrassed by going to see him twice in as many days.

When she stopped the buggy in front of the house, she saw that two of the windows were open—a good sign that he was most likely home.

After she had secured the horse, she headed to the front door. Before she reached it, she heard it creak open, and then she saw Nathan filling the frame of the doorway. He was grinning.

"Oh, hello," she said, not expecting him to be right there.

"Hi again, Violet." He pushed the door open wide. "Do you want to come inside?"

"Jah, I'd like that."

He left the door open and she walked in, following him to the living room, and then they both sat. It was a small room with two comfortable, soft brown couches. Over the back of each was a colorful crocheted blanket that his mother would've most likely made. Nathan sat in one and being too shy to sit too close, Violet sat in the one opposite.

"I was speaking with Valerie yesterday and she said she was coming here to see you."

"Jah, she did already and we talked about some things."

Violet nodded and clasped her hands tightly in her lap. "Good." There was an awkward silence. She glanced over at him and then her eyes flickered around the room, looking for something to talk about.

"Would you like tea or something?" he asked.

"Nee." She shook her head. "I need to get back home soon."

"I have to confess that I know nothing about funerals. *Mamm* looked after *Dat's* funeral. I feel bad that other people have taken over things that I should be doing." He ran a hand through his hair and she was glad he was finally talking just like when they were younger.

"It must be awful. I hate to even think about what you're going through."

"It's just that I'm feeling overwhelmed by everything. And I'm not normally like that. I'm normally in control." He shook his head. "I'm out of control at the moment." He gave a small laugh. "I have no idea what I'm doing or what I'm supposed to do."

"That's to be expected. No one knows how to do these things, I guess, until they have to do them."

"I've got so many decisions to make and it's not easy when my head's spinning."

Violet nodded, wishing she could put her arms around him to give him some form of comfort.

"It's just that I should've been here, Violet, you know?"

Violet stared at him, not knowing what to say. When she opened her mouth to say something, he spoke again.

"I should've moved back. She was sick, but I didn't

know she was going to die. If I'd known that, I would've come back and lived here with her. She's been sick before and gotten over it. Some days she was fine."

"Where did you go? I mean, where do you live now?"

"I've never gone far. I'm leasing a house in town with Abe and Ben."

Violet recognized the names of brothers who'd left the community after they'd been on their *rumspringas*.

"I came here every day during my lunch break to make sure she ate. I brought her food. I couldn't stay long, ten minutes or so. Then I came on the weekends to see her. Saturdays mostly because of the Sunday meetings."

She took the opportunity to say, "Well, you came every day to look after her; there wasn't much more you could've done."

"I could've moved back in."

"And she still would've been sick. You can't stop someone going when *Gott* calls them home."

He nodded. "But I would've been here. I could've given her comfort in those last few moments. Who was here with her when she died? No one. She died alone."

"I heard she went in her sleep—nice and peaceful."

"Maybe." He looked thoughtful. "That's what they said."

"*Gott* would've given her comfort. She wouldn't have been alone."

"Do you think so?" Nathan asked.

"I know it."

Nathan breathed out heavily. "I hope so."

"Nathan, can I ask you something?"

"Sure, anything."

"Why did you stop coming to the meetings?"

He took a while to respond. "I just felt like a few of

the folks in the community weren't respectful when my father was going through a hard time."

"What happened? Forgive me if I'm prying, I'm just interested to know."

"There was just too much judging and gossiping going on for my taste. I'm sure you heard the talk about my *daed?"*

She nodded uncomfortably. Violet had often heard the rumors and was embarrassed and felt horrible that Nathan and his mother knew that their father and husband were being talked about.

"Those rumors made my *mudder* feel like my *vadder* was not being a *gut* husband before he died. He had some problems, but he was trying. When he died, *Mamm* felt a lot of the people weren't the same to her. After that, not many people visited her. Sadly, I nearly became one of them." He looked around the room. "It's hard for me to stay in this *haus* for too long."

"Bad memories?"

"Yeah, bad memories, but not of my parents so much."

Violet nodded, knowing he meant that he had bad memories of the people in the community and how he'd perceived his father was treated.

"I just didn't want to come back and be around those people."

"I understand that people can be cruel and that's human nature, but you shouldn't let them stop you from worshipping and being close to *Gott,"* Violet said.

"I haven't stopped, Violet. I do worship; I just do it at home in my own way. I don't have to do it like the community says I should." There was a moment of silence, before Nathan asked, "Violet, why are you here?"

The question caught her off-guard. She hadn't expected him to ask. "Umm, I knew that this would be a hard time for anyone and I know you have no one to lean on. I figured that I could make this easier for you by being a friend. We were good friends when we went to *schul.*"

"What about how everyone feels about me? Aren't you afraid that they will treat you in the same way if they see you with me?" Nathan asked.

"If they do, then you're right about not wanting to be around them."

He nodded in acceptance of her answer.

Remembering Violet told Willow she wouldn't be too long, she rose to her feet. "I should get back home. They'll be wondering where I am."

"I appreciate you coming here and offering your friendship, and thank you for your letter. It makes me feel better to know I'll have you and Valerie there at the funeral tomorrow."

"You have many friends here."

Nathan scoffed. "I don't know about that."

"Hopefully, you'll find out just how many people care when you are at the funeral."

"Maybe." He walked her to the door.

When she walked past him onto the porch, she swung around. "Bye, Nathan."

"I'll see you at the funeral if I don't see you before."

She smiled at his words, and quickly faced the other direction so he would not see the color that she knew was rising to her cheeks. No man had ever made her feel like Nathan had. She was comfortable with him, but nervous at the same time. It was weird, and hard to explain, but he was different from any other man she'd ever known.

Things with Nathan were turning out far different than she had planned. She had to admit to herself that she liked him. It was as simple as that. Nathan was humble and strong, not to mention attractive. It might have been stubbornness that led him to leave the community.

As she rode home in the buggy, she blushed as she realized how brave she'd been to go there at all.

Nathan felt vastly different every time Violet was around. She gave him peace and renewed hope that everything would be okay. He hoped what she said would be true, that people would be friendly to him tomorrow at his mother's funeral. Maybe there were some community members who cared. He knew they weren't all bad; it was just that the horrid handful over shadowed all the good people.

He stayed in the doorway, leaning against it as he watched her buggy get smaller and smaller as it left him. He hoped there was more to her visit than her wanting to help and being a good friend. His greatest hope was that she liked him as more than a friend, but he knew a girl such as Violet would want a man with his two feet in the community. Not someone who had left and who had resentments in his heart.

Once Violet's buggy was out of sight, he closed his front door and sat down on the couch and closed his eyes. Before his face, he saw Violet with her perfectly-shaped oval face and the glasses that suited her and made her look interesting. She was a beautiful girl and he'd always liked her. He once had hopes that their friendship would blossom into something more. Now he saw that it probably never would. Even if she felt that same spark as he did, none of her family liked him. He was pretty sure she wouldn't go against what her family wanted for her.

He reached behind him, pulled one of his mother's handmade blankets over himself, and lay down. If he came back to the community, he'd have to forgive the people who'd said things about his father and thought less of his mother and him because of his father's actions. He wasn't ready to forgive. When he was younger, his mother taught him to accept people's apologies and tell them he forgave them even if he didn't.

She told him his heart would eventually catch up with his mouth where forgiveness was concerned. He didn't see how that could be true. What sense was it to let people say horrible things and then apologize after the hurt was carried out? Anyway, where was anyone's apology regarding him and his family being treated differently because of his father's shortcomings? Didn't God love everyone the same? It was no one's place to judge.

Right now, he had a comfortable life and wasn't ready to go back to the restrictions of the community.

Unfortunately for Violet, Willow hadn't been able to cover for her very well when she'd sneaked out to see Nathan. That was all too evident because as soon as she turned her buggy into the driveway, her mother was waiting for her with her feet planted firmly on the ground and hands on hips.

She slowed the horse when she got close to her mother.

"Where have you been?" her mother demanded.

Not wanting to tell a lie, Violet had no choice but to tell her the truth even though it was the last thing she wanted to do. "I went to visit Nathan."

Nerida's mouth opened wide. "You know how I feel about that. Come inside as soon as you can, and after dinner tonight, you and I are going to have a serious talk."

"Okay, *Mamm.*" She stopped still in the buggy and watched as her mother turned on her heel and stomped back into the house.

As she unhitched the buggy and tended the horse, she mentally ran through what her mother might say to her. She'd tell her why Nathan was totally unsuited and how there were so many other men around who'd be a far better match. Then she'd ask what young men she liked. Her mother was very similar to Aunt Nancy, her only sister.

She heard footsteps behind her and turned to see chubby-cheeks Willow huffing and puffing as she ran from the house to the barn.

"*Mamm* guessed where you were. I tried my hardest not to tell her."

"It's okay. She's already told me she's not happy I went to see him. She said I had to have a serious talk with her after dinner."

Willow's mouth dropped open. "I don't like the sound of that."

Violet grimaced and pushed her glasses higher on her nose. "Neither do I, but I could've gotten a worse punishment."

"I don't see why you're getting any punishment. You were only visiting a friend."

Violet finished rubbing down her horse and considered what Willow had said. The thing was she liked Nathan as more than a friend and that's obviously what her mother had guessed. Nathan would be the last man on her mother's list of potential suitors.

"Can I do anything to help?" Willow asked.

Violet straightened up. "You waited until I had nothing to do before you asked that."

Willow giggled. "Let's help *Mamm* with dinner and try to get her into a good mood."

"Good idea."

As they walked to the house, Violet said, "Isn't dinner started yet?"

"*Mamm* started on it and then asked me where you were. I tried not to tell her but you know how she can be. It was dreadful and I didn't want to get into trouble too."

Violet sighed. "It's okay, don't worry. I'll have to face what she says to me."

"We must try to get her into a good mood."

"Hmm, I don't know how we'll do with that."

Willow giggled. "I'll race you to the house." Willow took off running and Violet ran a little but her legs were still aching from all the walking she'd done recently. "I'm first. I get the prize," Willow said when she touched the side of the house.

"Yeah? What prize is that."

"I will think of something."

"You do that," Violet said, still worried about their mother. "You go in first."

Willow walked into the kitchen first, followed by Violet.

"I hope you've both washed your hands."

"We're just about to do that, *Mamm,*" Violet said.

"I'm all washed up," Willow said.

"*Gut.* You can help me cut these carrots while Violet washes up."

Violet and Willow's efforts didn't have much of an effect on their mother. She didn't smile once throughout dinner. Violet was starting to wonder if she was going to get grounded for going to see Nathan without telling her.

After dinner, Willow was left with cleaning the kitchen while Violet's father read the newspaper in the living room. Violet and her mother went to Violet's room to have their talk.

As they both sat down on the bed, Violet asked, "What's upset you most, *Mamm?*"

Her mother stared at her and blinked a couple of times. "Where should I start? Secret notes passed around, couriered by a young boy. Or should I start with you sneaking off to meet a boy without me knowing?"

Violet said, "It's not like what you're saying."

"Well, tell me exactly what it's like." Her mother was getting angrier.

"It's nothing to get upset about."

"I am upset. Do you like Nathan Beiler?"

"I do."

"As more than just a friend?" her mother asked.

Violet wasn't ready to share her feelings with her mother. "I'm not sure."

"Which young men do you like?"

"Mamm! Why are you asking me this? I don't feel comfortable telling you who I like and who I don't. Are you going to try and pair me with someone? Is that why you're asking?"

A gentle smile softened her mother's face. "I just want to make sure you don't make any mistakes and that you find the right man for you."

"I don't need your help finding a man. It will happen if and when it's meant to happen." Her mother's face soured when she told her that. It was as though that was the very last thing she had expected Violet to say.

"If?"

"Jah. Maybe not everyone is cut out to be married."

Her mother gasped and covered her mouth. "You can't be serious."

"I'm deadly serious." With one finger, Violet pushed her glasses further up her nose. "These specs would be off-putting to a man."

"Not the right man."

"So, you agree my glasses are ugly?" Violet huffed. "I should've gone with a different kind of frame. These ones stand out too much and they're too heavy. They keep falling down my nose."

"They might need an adjustment."

"I'll adjust them right into the trashcan. They're ugly." Violet figured she would rather talk to her mother about her glasses than talk to her about a man.

"They're not ugly, they bring out your eyes."

"You mean they make my eyes look bigger because they're magnified? I'm like a goggle-eyed fish."

"You're not! You're just as lovely as before. You've never complained about wearing them until now. Did someone say something?"

Violet shook her head. *"Nee,* don't worry."

"I want you to talk to me about things."

Violet sighed. "It's not easy sometimes because we think so differently about things."

"As far as your glasses are concerned, you need them and should be grateful for them. Your *vadder* paid good money for them."

"Sorry, *Mamm.* I'm grateful for them."

Nathan had finally managed to get some sleep the night before his mother's funeral. He'd stayed awake thinking about everything from his younger days when he'd been happy, before his father turned to drink, to recent times with Violet.

He hoped the day wouldn't be too stressful, but he was saying goodbye to his mother, so he knew it would be an emotional time. At least now his mother was at peace and out of pain.

If the people he was annoyed with showed up, he wouldn't let them bother him. He'd ignore them and if they talked to him he'd be polite and keep focused on the reason he was there.

Still in bed, he stretched his arms over his head and yawned. It was time to wake up now and get himself to the bishop's house where the viewing of his mother's body was to be held.

The bishop and his wife had been wonderful to him since his mother died. He'd always gotten along with them and respected not only the bishop but all the church oversight. It was some of the other people who'd been talking meanly about his father. Although it was the bishop who'd made the decision regarding all the shunnings his father got over the years, Nathan didn't hold that against him because he believed he was doing that for a Godly purpose. Although the bishop should've been at Nathan's house to see how unbearable that made things in the home over that period.

Nathan wouldn't have been able to handle the viewing as well as all the Amish people who would be coming to say goodbye to his mother. She had to have an Amish funeral and that was something he wasn't able to do by himself. It was thanks to people like Valerie that his mother was having a good send off.

Before he got out of bed, he thought about what his

mother had wanted for his life. When he'd seen her lying there sick and helpless, he'd led her to believe he'd return to the community one day, get married, and have lots of children. He had to let her think that. Now that Violet had come back into his life, a part of him thought that the things he'd told his mother might become a reality.

Nathan got out of bed and changed into the clothes that he'd laid out for himself the night before. He'd purchased a plain black suit for the occasion and teamed it with a white long-sleeved shirt. He already owned a pair of black lace-up shoes.

After he got dressed, he had an uncanny sense of his mother's presence. It felt like she was right there in front of him. He sat down on the couch for a few moments and closed his eyes. He hadn't thought of eternity in a long time or where he could end up spending it. Nathan believed in God, but he wasn't convinced that the Amish way was the only way to be right with God. Although he had to admit it was easier to follow God within the confines of the community as the temptations of the world weren't there every day to distract him.

He sat and waited for Ed Bontrager, who was collecting him to take him to the bishop's house. He didn't think it was appropriate to arrive at his mother's funeral in a car. It was much better to arrive in a buggy with a member of the Amish community. All the while, his stomach rumbled, but he was far too nervous to eat a thing.

Chapter Six

As Violet rode along to the bishop's house for the viewing prior to the funeral, she leaned forward, closer to her mother, who was sitting in the front seat of the family buggy. "Do you know who's taking Nathan? Is someone collecting him?"

Her father turned toward her and said, "Ed Bontrager is collecting him."

Violet leaned back in the seat. She guessed that had to be Valerie's doing since she was close to Ed. When she sensed Willow staring at her, she looked over at her and then Willow looked away. Willow didn't like her being friendly with Nathan even though she was trying to be better about it. She basically had the same opinion of Nathan as her mother had—that he was no good.

She wondered what her father thought of Nathan. She wasn't about to ask, not in the presence of her mother and sister.

When they arrived at the bishop's house, they pulled alongside the house and past the row of buggies. Nerida had a bad leg and couldn't walk far. It had been broken some time ago and had given her trouble ever since.

"You lot get out here," Violet's father said.

Violet helped her mother out and then her father turned the buggy around and headed to park it at the end of one of the many rows of buggies.

Together they walked into the house and the first thing Violet saw was the coffin as people filed past it for the viewing. When she walked further inside, she saw Nathan to one side of the long living area, standing next to Ed Bontrager.

His face lit up when their eyes met and she walked over to him.

"Hello, Nathan."

"Hi, Violet."

"How are you feeling?"

"Just as you'd expect someone would feel at their mother's funeral, I'd reckon. I'll get through it."

She looked across at Ed and he looked happy to stay by Nathan's side, keeping him company.

"Everyone's been really good," Nathan added. "I've appreciated everyone's support. People have said lovely things to me about my mother, and me—surprisingly."

"Probably because they found out how you stopped by every day to look after her even when you were working long hours."

"Well, she was my mother. I didn't stay that long anyway. Just in my lunch hour."

"I know that, but people had somehow gotten the opposite impression and thought you never visited and stayed away."

He shrugged. "I dunno."

Ed Bontrager said, "People often get the wrong impression about things. If you'll excuse me, I see someone I need to talk with." He walked away, leaving Violet and Nathan alone.

"I suppose there's a lot of people here that you haven't seen for a long time?" Violet asked.

"*Jah,* people haven't really changed—in looks I mean. Everyone seems to be the same, just a little older."

Soon, Violet was edged out of the way as other people came up to see Nathan. Violet was pleased that people were making the effort to make Nathan feel comfortable.

When she saw Molly Gingerich glaring at Nathan from the other side of the room, she thought she should know the truth about Nathan.

"Hello, Mrs. Gingerich."

"Oh, it's you, Violet. Did you have those glasses before?"

"I had them on the other day when I came to your *haus.*"

"I didn't notice them."

"I thought you should know that Nathan came to his *mudder's haus* every day to see how she was."

"Is that true?"

"*Jah.* It's true."

"Hmm. That would explain a few things. I've misjudged the boy."

"He's a man now."

She looked over at him. "*Jah,* he is. I must speak to him."

Molly walked away from her without saying a word.

When she saw Molly and Nathan talking, Violet then walked over to Willow and stayed by her until the men came to take the coffin outside. Everyone in the bishop's house stopped still and watched the coffin being taken out of the house, carried on the shoulders of four men.

Assuming that Nathan would continue on to the graveyard in Ed's buggy, she didn't invite Nathan to go in the buggy with her family.

The coffin was then placed in the long, specially-constructed black funeral buggy. The buggy carrying the coffin went first, followed by the regular buggies. Violet's family was in the very last buggy. Their father had parked far away and he had to drive up to the house for his wife's sake to collect her so she wouldn't have far to walk.

When they reached the graveyard, Violet was the first of her family out of the buggy, as she wanted to make sure Nathan wasn't alone.

She walked along, following the crowd, and saw Nathan standing next to the bishop. They were talking and looking down at the coffin by the open grave. Old Mrs. Gingerich was there too, on the other side, wiping her tears away with a white handkerchief.

As much as she was sad for Mrs. Gingerich, Violet was pleased that everyone had seemed to rally around Nathan. He would surely get over this feeling that many in the community disapproved of him. No one could blame him for his father's actions and think that was a reasonable thing to do.

When everybody had arrived and was gathered at the grave, the bishop read out a hymn and then offered a lengthy prayer while four men lowered the coffin into the freshly-dug grave.

Word had spread that the meal afterwards would be held at Valerie's house. While she was staring at Nathan, who was transfixed on the grave right by the bishop's side, Violet's father walked up to her. "Come on, Violet. We'll go to Valerie's *haus.*"

"Give me a moment, *Dat,*" she said, still staring at Nathan.

Her father stood silently by her side until she felt uncomfortable about what her father might think about her staring at Nathan. She looked up at her father. "I'm ready to go now, *Dat.*"

Her father put his arm loosely around her shoulder and led her back to the buggy.

When they were driving away, she stared back at Nathan to see him speaking to the bishop. They seemed to be getting along well.

Nathan was pleased that Mrs. Gingerich had said some kind words. She'd even apologized for thinking bad things about him. She made him give his word he'd say goodbye to her before he left his mother's house for good. Then he looked at the bishop, who was standing by his side. "Thank you for everything you've done today, Bishop John."

The bishop's lips turned upward above his long, graying black beard. "Your *mudder* was a valued member of the community. Now she's home."

"I know, and she's out of pain and at peace. I miss her dreadfully."

The bishop nodded. "We all miss those who have gone before us. Just know that you have a home here and everyone here is your family. We're ready to accept you when you're ready to come back, Nathan."

The bishop's words touched him greatly. He felt tears coming to his eyes and he blinked them back. "Thank you, that means a lot. I have thought about it more seriously in these past few days."

"That's good. I'm surprised you left when you did. I always thought you would stay with us."

He thought he should tell the bishop what was on his heart. "To be totally open with you, I didn't like how some people treated my father. I was angry about that and that's why I left. I just couldn't understand it."

"When he was shunned?" the bishop asked.

"When he was shunned and then before and after he was shunned. Pretty much all the time. I just thought people were treating us as if we weren't good enough, or were somehow different and separate to them."

"Maybe they were scared of being affected by what your *vadder* was doing."

Nathan didn't think that was true. "I don't know. It was more like they were being judgmental and a bit nasty." He scratched his head, hoping he hadn't offended the bishop or overstepped the mark.

"None of us is perfect, Nathan. And by judging them, you yourself become judgmental."

Nathan had to chuckle. "I hadn't thought of it like that."

"We're each responsible for our own walk with God. And that's too important to take your eyes off *Gott* to look around to see what others are doing. Keep focused on what you're doing because that's what's important. Think of things this way. It doesn't matter what men say or think about us and if they treat us badly it's okay. As long as we're in right standing with *Gott,* none of the rest matters." He patted Nathan on the back.

"I understand." Nathan looked down at the dirt on the ground underneath his black shoes. For the first time, it didn't matter what others said or thought about him. What the bishop had said had changed his point of view completely. Maybe those people were scared or maybe they were just plain mean, but he wouldn't let them affect his walk with God. Maybe he could return to the community. Maybe he could have the life that his mother had always hoped for him. Before his eyes, standing right there talking to the bishop, he had a flash of a future—a happy one with Violet and loads of children.

Valerie had gone on with someone else and Ed had stayed behind to bring Nathan to the meal afterward. With everyone going to so much effort, Nathan couldn't say that the people in the community didn't care.

Violet made herself busy helping the ladies set the food out on two long tables.

When Nathan eventually walked into the house, his face looked as white as a sheet.

It seemed Violet was not the only one who had noticed because, before she could make a move, Valerie was by his side, pulling him over to sit on one of the chairs that lined the walls.

Someone else passed Nathan a glass of soda and Violet decided to leave it awhile before she went over to him, but she still never took her eyes from him. Later, when he looked up and saw her, he smiled and she was drawn to him.

She sat down on the seat beside him. "I was going to come and talk to you earlier, but everyone else had the same idea."

He chuckled and looked down at the drink in his hands.

"Everyone's been good, especially you, Valerie, and the bishop. I'll never forget how good you all have been to me. This is the hardest thing I've had to deal with in my life."

"I saw you talking to the bishop earlier."

"Yes, I told him what's in my heart and he had some answers that I hadn't expected. He made me look at things differently."

"That's good."

Nathan nodded. "What he said made a lot of sense."

Violet hoped that the contact with the community members would prompt Nathan to re-attend the gatherings. "Anything you want to share with me?"

He chuckled. "Not today."

When other people approached Nathan, Violet excused herself and went to help Valerie in the kitchen.

As the day of the funeral drew to a close and people started to leave Valerie's house, Violet's parents came to tell her it was time to go.

"I'll be home soon. I'm just going to help Valerie clean up." Violet hoped her voice was firm enough so they wouldn't argue with her. "Maybe I'll walk home later."

"That isn't your job; you aren't his *fraa.*" Her father frowned at her. "Get your things and come with us; there are plenty of ladies here to help clean up."

"Dat, I'm helping Valerie."

"Let's go," her father said in a hushed tone.

"Okay. I'll just say goodbye to a few people." Not wanting to make her parents upset, she hurried over to Nathan.

"I have to go home, Nathan. I wanted to stay and help Valerie, but…"

"I understand. You've been wonderful today. Thank you. I hope I'll see you again soon."

"Violet, come on," her father urged.

"I must go." Violet hurried back to her father. "I'll just tell Valerie I'm going."

He nodded and didn't look happy.

She found Valerie in the kitchen. "I wanted to stay on and help, but I'm told I must go home and go home now."

Valerie chuckled. "Bye, Violet. You've been a good help today. I'm sure Nathan appreciated it."

"Bye, Valerie." She hurried to her parents, who had already walked out of the house.

Violet was silent on the ride home, struggling to understand why her parents had made her leave.

"We allowed you to help that man while he was grieving, but now that the funeral is over, I don't want you anywhere near him," her mother said.

Violet knew she should never argue with her mother when she used that tone, but she felt compelled to speak her mind. *"Mamm,* I mean no disrespect, but I'm no longer a child. I can speak to whomever I want. Nathan still needs help. The funeral being over doesn't mean he'll forget how hard it is to lose his *mudder."*

Her mother turned around and wagged her finger at her. "I'll not have you take that tone with me. You're still my *dochder.*"

Her father took over the lecture. "Spending time with that man has already had an ill effect on you. The Scripture says that you should be mindful of those you spend time with. He is not a member of our community and shows no sign of returning."

"He could come back and I don't want people standing in his way. The bishop has been nice to him. Nathan told me he had a good talk with him today and if the bishop is nice to him, shouldn't both of you be? Or you could be judged for standing in a sinner's way."

From the back seat of the buggy, she could see the tips of her *vadder's* ears turning beet red. Perhaps she should've thought through her words before she said them. "Forgive me, *Dat.*"

"As long as you're an unmarried woman, still living in our *haus*, you will not see that man again. Your *mudder* told me how you sneaked out of the house yesterday to see him and had young Toby Yoder passing secret letters. This is a small community, and I'll not allow you to embarrass us."

Her *mudder* nodded in agreement and turned around to stare at her. Violet nodded and then her mother turned back around.

Exactly how was she embarrassing them by associating with Nathan? She knew she risked her father's wrath if she continued on the subject, but nevertheless, she forged ahead. *"Dat,* he isn't a criminal. How am I embarrassing you?"

"He's an outcast, as *gut* as shunned, and as long as you are seen with him, you will be too."

"He can't be shunned if he's never been baptized. He's never made the decision to join us."

Her mother turned around, stared at her, and said, "Why don't you listen to your own words?"

"What do you mean?" Violet felt sick with this confrontation, but she felt she had to stick up for Nathan.

Her father bought into the conversation. "You just said he's never made the decision to join us."

"Jah, I know."

Her father continued, "Don't you see a problem with that? He's had enough time and he's done nothing."

"Well, have you ever wondered why he left and stopped coming to the gatherings?" Violet asked, risking more of her *vadder's* anger.

"Nee, I've too much to do to wonder about what others think."

It was no use talking to her father. Maybe her parents were amongst the people who had let Nathan down in the past. That was a horrible thought. She tried to clear Nathan from her mind. She tried to erase the feelings that had grown in her during the brief moments she had spent with him.

There was no way Violet could forget Nathan. Violet was falling in love with him, and she believed he felt the same—he had to have those same feelings. She could see it in the way he looked at her, especially today at the funeral. There was no way she could just pretend that he no longer existed. She closed her eyes tightly and right there in the back seat of the buggy, she prayed that he would return. And if and when he did, she hoped that her parents wouldn't stand in his way of feeling comfortable and a part of the community.

Chapter Seven

The next day, Violet's life returned to normal. She got up early to deliver flowers to the markets as she did three days a week. On the mornings she was working, she loaded a wagon with flowers from the Walkers' greenhouses and took them to the markets.

Violet's workday was split into a morning shift and an evening one, and she had free time in the middle of the day. Lily worked in the flower stall at the markets five and a half days a week. The Walkers ran a wholesale flower business. They lived next door to her Aunt Nancy, and it seemed each of her cousins had worked there at one time or another.

As Violet unloaded the flowers that morning, Lily arrived.

"Gut mayrie, Lily."

"Hi there. I'm so looking forward to the dinner."

"What dinner is this?" Violet asked.

"It's the dinner for *Dat's* birthday. Everyone's coming. I don't know why you haven't heard about it. It's next Thursday."

"Your *vadder* doesn't normally have a big birthday."

"I know, but for some reason *Mamm* and Aunt Nerida are making this one a special one."

Violet stopped what she was doing and straightened up. "Is he having a birthday that ends with a zero?"

"Nee. He's fifty-eight."

"Hmmm." Violet had to wonder whether this dinner was solely for her benefit.

"Hey, what's wrong?"

Violet shook her head. "It's nothing." Violet turned away and continued lifting the buckets of flowers onto the display.

"I know you're all invited. *Mamm* was talking to Aunt Nerida about it just yesterday."

"It's not that. I wasn't thinking that we weren't invited. It's just that…"

"What?"

"Nothing. I'm just having a hard time at the moment with *Mamm* and *Dat.* They're being really strict."

"Do you want to come and stay with me for a while?" Lily asked.

"Could I?"

"Jah, if you want to. Elijah won't mind and it'll give me someone to sit with of an evening. Elijah always goes to bed so early and I'm by myself now that Bruno and Daisy are away with Bruno's *familye* in Ohio."

The identical twins, Daisy and Lily, lived in houses side by side on the same piece of land. And now Violet knew they also spent a lot of time in each other's houses. They were still as close as they could be.

"Denke, Lily. I'd love that. I hope I'm allowed."

"Of course you will be. Do you want me to ask Aunt Nerida? I'll say I'm lonely and I need you around for some company." Lily giggled. "And it's the truth. I think if I ask Aunt Nerida, she'll say you can stay."

This was just what Violet needed, time away from her parents. "I'd be so grateful if you would do that."

"Gut. That's settled. I'll call her when I'm having my morning break."

"It's her day to come to the markets, so you might see her soon."

"Even better. Don't worry about a thing. We all need a break from our parents every now and again."

"I could certainly use time away from them right now. We haven't been getting along too well." Glancing over at the remaining buckets of flowers, Violet said, "Willow mightn't be too happy about me going."

"Just be concerned about yourself for the moment. Willow will survive. You probably need a break from her too."

Violet nodded, thinking she needed time away from everyone. "Maybe. Are you sure Elijah won't mind?"

"He'll be fine. He never says no to anything I want and you can use my buggy while I'm at work and go anywhere you want."

"Really?"

"Jah."

Happiness flooded through Violet's body as she thought of the total freedom she'd have without having to tell her parents where she was at every moment of every day. *"Denke,* Lily. You're so kind."

"It's more for me than it is for you. I told you I need the company. You'll have to talk to me a lot of the evenings because Elijah says I talk too much."

Violet giggled. "I can talk to you and I'll listen to what you say too."

Lily threw her arms around Violet's waist and hugged her tight. "I can't wait."

"Me either. Let me know what my *mudder* says."

"I'll try to have an answer by the time you get back this afternoon."

"Denke."

Violet invested her energy into unloading the rest of the flowers. A break at Lily's house away from her parents sounded like just the thing she needed.

"Have you told her about the birthday party yet?" Nerida asked as she breathlessly burst into Nancy's kitchen later that day.

Nancy had been humming while kneading bread on the kitchen table.

Nancy jumped. "Oh, you gave me a fright." Her sister often barged into the house without knocking. It annoyed Nancy, but she didn't say anything. She was just pleased that they were back on speaking terms again after the dreadful rift they'd had that lasted years.

"Sorry, I didn't mean to scare you. I saw the door open and came right in."

"That's all right. I was just lost in my own world. Were you talking about telling Violet about Hezekiah's birthday dinner?"

"*Jah.* That's right."

"*Nee.* She's your *dochder.* You should tell her about it."

"*Nee,* because then she'd think of a reason not to come if I mentioned it. John and I haven't been getting along with her very well at the moment. John doesn't like all the attention she's been giving Nathan. If she thought we wanted her to go somewhere, she probably wouldn't. You know how stubborn she is, don't you?"

"Jah, it runs in the *familye."* Nancy frowned at her sister, trying to make sense of what she'd just said, then she added, "You tell her, only don't call it a party. If she thinks a lot of people will be there, or that it's a party, she won't want to come. She'd want to come to her *onkel's* birthday dinner."

"That's a good idea, so sensible. I'll tell everyone to call it a dinner. I don't know why we started calling it a party. Anyway, I stopped by to tell you that our plans might already be heading south." Nerida's body trembled.

"What do you mean?" Nancy asked.

"I was at the markets and Lily said she'd asked Violet if she could stay at her *haus* for a few weeks while Daisy's away."

Nancy tapped a finger on her chin. "If she was any other girl, I'd think she'd organized that with Lily so she would be closer to a man."

Nerida took a step closer to her sister. "You mean she might have an ulterior motive for staying with Lily?"

"Exactly," Nancy said, turning her attention back to the dough. Once again, she dusted her hands lightly with flour and then she arranged the dough into loaf tins.

"Nee, she's not like that," Nerida said, looking annoyed that Nancy would think such a thing of her daughter.

Nancy shut the oven door and stood straight. "What are your thoughts on Nathan Beiler?"

Nerida gasped and put a hand on her chest. "You don't think she's sneaking away to see *him,* do you?

She's already done that once. At least she admitted to it, I suppose, so she couldn't have been doing anything bad."

"*Nee.* I'm not saying that, Nerida. You do get carried away by things."

Nerida shook her head. "I told her to keep away from Nathan and so did John. She wouldn't disobey us. We had a big talk with her about him."

"Tell me what you think is wrong with him."

"We told her not to talk to him unless he comes back to the community properly. There's nothing exactly wrong with him as a person; it's just that he's not one of us. He's not a member of the community. You see, he's had plenty of time to return, but he hasn't bothered."

"Why does she want to stay with Lily? Maybe a man is involved and it could be someone other than Nathan."

Nerida tapped a finger on her chin. "Violet's not a devious girl. She wouldn't have a reason other than Lily asked her to stay there. Lily told me Elijah goes to bed early and she stays up alone. She's missing Daisy, she said. That could be right and there could be nothing more to it."

Nancy sighed. "Where does that leave our plans?"

"You're the expert, Nancy. You tell me."

"We'll work out who's a good match for her and we'll plan things from there. We'll turn it to our advantage that she's staying with Lily. She'll be out of our way and she won't suspect a thing." Nancy chuckled.

"I wish I had your confidence."

"Trust me. I managed to get all four of my *dochders* married, even the twins."

Nerida nodded. "That was impressive. I don't mean

to be rude about the twins, but before they were married they were a little…"

"A little unfocused?"

"Jah. That wasn't quite what I was going to say, but I didn't think they would get married until they were a lot older."

"Marriage matured them."

"Jah, and it's nice that the two of them found a way to stay close."

"Gott always blesses us with what we want when we're following His ways."

"Jah, they are blessed. I hope my girls find lovely men too. What's your secret with matching people together?"

"I found someone I liked for each of the girls and then arranged for them to be together more often than they normally would. Things progressed naturally from there. I just gave everything a helping hand. I can't take credit for finding Bruno, though. He was a nice surprise, and what better husband for one of my *dochders* than Valerie's younger *bruder?"*

"I'd have to agree on that. Now where's that list I gave you?"

"I'll get it." Nancy leaned over and looked at the four loaf tins in the oven before she retrieved the list.

As Nerida gazed over the names on the list, she said, "We should pick someone ourselves, since she hasn't shown any preference toward one person over another."

"I know." Nancy clapped her hands together. "I have the perfect man in mind. Benjamin Hostetler, and he's a good friend of Elijah's. Violet could easily see a lot more of him now that she's staying at Elijah and Lily's *haus."*

"That would be perfect. I know he comes from a good family. What's he like? I've never spoken to him."

"He's *wunderbaar.* Do you want to meet him before we make plans?"

"My only concern is that he'll take Violet away somewhere with him. I know he comes from a small community just outside of Ohio. Or has he moved here permanently?"

"He's here to stay, I've heard, and we should move quickly. I don't know why I didn't think of him before."

"I think we should wait. I'd like to meet him first and see what I think. Is he on the list for Hezekiah's birthday dinner?"

"He is now." Nancy laughed as she tapped a finger on the list. Once she sat down with it, she took up a pen and scribbled his name on the bottom. "Nerida, do you think we should invite Nathan?"

Nerida sat down. *"Nee."*

"Wait and listen to my thoughts before you get all bossy."

Nerida huffed. "Why would it be a good idea to invite him?"

"If we don't, Violet might focus on him too much and since she knows you and John disapprove of him, it might drive her to him."

Slowly, Nerida nodded. "I see where you're going. Invite him and then let her see for herself that he falls short of the other young men who are there. I know she's a sensible girl."

Nancy nodded. "We'll just have him there in the mix. What do you think?"

"Okay." Nerida's face soured.

"What's wrong now? Do you think he's that bad?"

"It's not that he's bad, but I don't want Violet having the burden of being with a man who might suddenly leave the community. We don't even know if he's come back to stay. No one knows if he's in or he's out. Violet needs someone with some solid reliability, someone stable."

"It'll work out. Trust me. I'll stop by and invite him myself. He's at Lorraine's *haus.* Well, I suppose it's his place now."

Nerida sighed. *"Jah,* it's best that you invite him and I hope John sees the sense in all this."

"He will, trust me," Nancy said.

Instead of take-out like he'd had nearly every night for the past week, Nathan had decided to cook himself a decent meal. Nathan was busy cutting up his vegetables for dinner when he heard a buggy. He looked out the window to see Nancy Yoder and she was by herself. There was no Valerie. He finished cutting the carrot and then pushed the vegetables to one side and walked out to see what Nancy wanted.

By the time he got to the door, Nancy was standing there just about to knock.

"Hi, Nancy."

"Hello, Nathan."

"Please come in." He stepped aside to allow her through.

"What have you been doing?"

"I was just cutting some vegetables for dinner. I've been having a lot of take-out lately. Have a seat."

When they were both sitting on the couch, she said, "I've come to invite you to Hezekiah's birthday dinner. He's having a big birthday this year."

Nathan wondered how old he was. Fifty, or perhaps even sixty? He didn't like to guess and nor did he like to ask. It was unusual for the Amish to make a big deal out of birthdays. "Thank you. It's very nice of you to ask me."

"I didn't ask you out of politeness. I asked because I really wanted you to come. Will you?"

"When is it on?"

Nancy told him the date. It wasn't too far away.

"Okay, thank you. Is it okay if I think about it? It's just that…" He sighed. "I don't know. I guess I've got a few things to sort out."

Nancy smiled. "Did I mention there'll be lots of food there?"

He chuckled. "I am fond of my food."

"All men are."

"I guess so."

"You don't even have to let me know. If you decide to come, just turn up."

Nathan knew that was the Amish way. No one ever gave RSVPs or expected them. The invitation made Nathan feel welcomed and accepted. Acceptance from Violet's close relations was a good thing. Maybe he could return and feel at home in the community. For the first time, he had a glimmer of hope that he could find his way back.

"The funeral went well," Nancy said.

"Yes, it was good to see the people I haven't seen in so long. My mother would have liked it."

"She would've." Nancy looked around her. "What are you going to do with the *haus?*"

Nathan was a little surprised by her question. It showed that she thought he wasn't coming back, and if she thought that, why was she inviting him to Hezekiah's birthday dinner? "I'm not sure what I'm going to do as yet. It depends on a few things."

"*Jah,* I suppose it would. I hope you don't mind me asking."

"I don't. I guess it's only natural to wonder about these practicalities of life."

Nancy nodded. "I should get back to get the dinner on and see what Hezekiah is doing."

"Okay. *Denke* once again for inviting me. I guess you'll have a lot of people there?"

"It'll be big. I've invited everyone we know." Nancy stood up and Nathan followed her to the door.

"Bye, Nancy."

When she was through the doorway, she turned around to face him. "Is there anything I can do for you, Nathan?"

"No thank you. Everything is fine. You and Valerie have done more than enough already."

"Okay, well, don't hesitate to ask if you think of anything."

"Thanks again, Nancy."

Nancy smiled at him and gave a little wave before she climbed into her buggy. He watched Nancy's horse clip-clopping away from his house, and then he headed back inside to continue chopping his vegetables for dinner.

Chapter Eight

That evening, Elijah and Lily arrived to collect Violet to stay with them.

"Denke for coming to collect her. It's saved me a trip out there," Violet's father, John, said when he opened the front door to them both.

Elijah smiled. "It's not far for us to go."

"Are you ready?" Lily asked Violet, who was standing behind her father.

"Jah, I've got my bag by the door."

Nerida stepped forward. "How are you going to get to and from work?"

"It's all organized, *Mamm.* Don't worry. I'm not a child anymore." She looked over at Lily and laughed. "Come on, let's get out of here before she asks me if I'm taking enough to wear and if I'll be warm enough."

"Well, are you taking enough clothes? I'm doing the washing tomorrow and I can drop some more over to you if you need some."

Violet shook her head. "Goodbye, *Mamm."*

"Well, why did you mention clothes?"

A small voice came from the living room. "Goodbye, Violet."

"Bye, Willow. I'll be back before you know it."

Willow was sitting on the couch in the living room, sewing with a blanket over her knees. When she didn't look up from her sampler, Violet knew she was sad about her going, but this was something she needed to do.

As soon as they were out of the house, Elijah took Violet's bag and then Lily walked with her to the buggy.

"What's going on with you two—you and Aunt Nerida?"

"You could tell there was something wrong?"

"It was obvious. You were tense with each other and you haven't been like that before."

"Didn't I tell you? They're getting all strict on me and I haven't even done anything wrong."

"Time apart will do you all good."

Lily and Violet climbed into the buggy while Elijah put Violet's bag in the back.

That night, Violet stayed up late talking to Lily.

When Violet finally went up to the small spare room, she sat on the edge of the bed. The room was small and fitted only a double bed and a small dresser. The walls were pale yellow with the same color curtains—hand sewn by Lily.

Violet noticed the quilt on the bed. It was beautifully sewn with small stitches. The stitches looked like they'd been done by hand rather than on a treadle or gas-powered sewing machine. The sections were all different shades of yellow and green. Then Violet recalled a long time ago that the twins, Daisy and Lily, had worked on that quilt as children. Violet had never associated much with the cousins when they were all growing up. It was due to the rift that had developed between her mother and Aunt Nancy. Maybe her mother had been harsh with Nancy just like she'd been harsh about Nathan.

For some reason, Violet couldn't get Nathan out of her mind. Everything reminded her of him.

Violet woke early the next morning and found Lily in the kitchen making breakfast.

"Elijah's just left," Lily explained as she continued to fiddle with the coffee machine that sat atop the gas stove. "Do you want *kaffe?"*

"Jah, please. Can I help with anything?"

"Nee, sit down and I'll fix you some breakfast."

Once Violet was sitting, Lily said, "Elijah invited someone for dinner tonight. I hope you don't mind. I know you came here for a quiet time."

"It's your *haus.* Just do what you normally do. Who's coming?" She desperately hoped that Lily might say Elijah had invited Nathan.

"It's Benjamin Hostetler."

Her heart sank and she tried her best to cover up her disappointment. "Okay."

"Do you know him?"

"Jah, I talked to him a few Sundays ago. He seems nice."

"He's been here a few times. Elijah and he get along well."

Lily glanced at the clock.

"What time do we have to leave?" asked Violet. "I don't know how long it takes from here."

"In about fifteen minutes."

"That's early."

"I know," said Lily.

"I can come and get you after I collect the flowers."

"Nee. I'll take you to the Walkers' and then I'll see if I can leave my horse and buggy there until evening; then you can take me to the flower stall, and collect me in the wagon at the end of the day. You can use my buggy in the middle of the day while I'm working."

Lily talked so much that she'd forgotten she'd already offered Violet use of the buggy during the day. "Okay. That sounds good."

Violet felt better being around Lily. The four of her female cousins had become like big sisters to her over the past few years. The eldest of the sisters, Rose and Tulip, now had children, but Lily and Daisy still didn't have any. She wondered if that upset them. Most couples had children arrive within the first year or two of marriage.

While Nathan ate his tasteless dinner of pan-fried chicken and vegetables, he gave some thought to his future. Now with both his mother and father gone, he felt empty. It wasn't fun to be alone in the quiet house. He considered coming back to the community and being surrounded by a close circle of people. From what he'd seen at the funeral, there would be people he could get along with. Many people had gone out of their way to be friendly to him.

Right now, he had a more pressing need to get back to the real world. At least he had his housemates who had become his close friends. He couldn't leave without saying goodbye to the two people who'd been the nicest to him and that was Valerie and Violet. Since it was still early in the evening, he figured he'd stop by and say goodbye to both of them. Then he remembered he'd told Molly Gingerich he'd say goodbye before he left.

Nathan knocked on Molly Gingerich's door and she opened it.

"Nathan, come in."

"I won't, thanks, Mrs. Gingerich. It's late for visiting. I just wanted to say goodbye and let you know I'm leaving my Mom's house to go back home."

"I hoped you'd stick around a little longer."

"I've got to get back to work and it's too far from Mom's house. I could do it, but I just need to get back to my routine."

"I understand. Will you stop by every now and again?"

He nodded. "I will. Thank you again for being a good friend to my mother. I know my mother was grateful for your visits. She talked about you often."

Molly chuckled. "She was a good woman and a good friend."

They smiled at one another and then Nathan said, "I'll see you soon. I'm not sure when, though."

"Okay. *Denke* for coming to see me."

He stepped away. "Bye, Mrs. Gingerich."

"Bye."

He got in his car and drove away, heading to Violet's house. He left his car a distance from the house in case they didn't appreciate having a vehicle parked so close.

After he knocked, Violet's mother opened the door.

"Hello." She didn't even have a hint of a smile on her face and that made him uneasy.

"Hello. I'm sorry to come at this late hour, but I

wondered if I might have a quick word with Violet to say goodbye."

Her expression changed immediately. "You're going?"

"Yes, I'm going back home where I belong."

"Oh, well Violet's not here."

"Do you mind me asking where I might find her?"

"Nathan, I'll let her know you were kind enough to stop by and say goodbye." She went to close the door.

"I'd really like to know where she is so I can say goodbye in person. She's been really good to me and very kind. I feel I owe her that much." He stared at her, willing her to let him know where he could find Violet. Just when it looked like she was weakening, her face returned to its former hardness.

"Like I said, I'll tell her you stopped by. Goodbye, Nathan." She closed the door.

He turned around and as he walked to the car, he knew he couldn't leave. Not without seeing her just one more time. He'd change his plans and stay another night at his mother's home. When he had his hand on the car door handle, he saw movement coming from the house. It was Violet's chubby younger sister running toward him.

He walked toward her. "Hi, Willow."

"She's at Lily and Elijah's."

"Violet?"

"Jah." Willow glanced nervously over her shoulder.

She'd clearly gone against her parents' wishes by giving him that information. If he'd done that when his father was still alive, he would've been taken out by the barn and given a whipping. "Why?"

"Why am I telling you, or why is she at Lily's *haus?"*

"Why are you telling me?"

"I feel it's the right thing to do."

"Thank you."

Willow glanced back at the house again and this time her father was striding toward them. "You should go now, Nathan. She'll be at the markets tomorrow morning too."

"Willow!" her father called out.

"Coming, *Dat.*"

"Thanks again, Willow," Nathan said.

Willow turned back to Nathan. "Just go! Quick!"

Nathan jumped back in his car, feeling bad for Willow.

When Nathan knocked on the door, it opened immediately and he saw Valerie's smiling face. She'd never had any children and lately Nathan had thought that was a shame because she would've made a wonderful mother. Valerie had a kind heart just like his mother had.

"Come in, Nathan."

"Thanks, Valerie."

"Have you had dinner?"

"Yes. I cooked it myself. I don't do much cooking. One of my housemates usually does all the cooking."

"It's not hard to cook."

He shrugged his shoulders. "Everything I've ever cooked has tasted dreadful."

"You probably need to be shown a few basic things. I could help you."

"I don't think I'll be sticking around long enough, but thanks."

"Would you like dessert? I was just about to have some. I have fruit salad and custard with apple pie."

He chuckled. "I won't say no to that."

Valerie laughed. "Come into the kitchen. I'll fix us some."

While Valerie cut the pie, he finally talked about the reason he was there. "I'm thinking of going back home tomorrow night."

Valerie looked up. "Really?"

"Yeah, I have to go some time. I need to get back into a proper routine and *Mamm's* house is a distance from where I work. It's not that far but the house I share with a couple of guys is much closer."

"That's a shame. I was hoping you'd surprise us all and stay on."

Nathan didn't know what to say. He was grateful to have some friends in the community.

Valerie continued, "Still, it's your decision."

"You never know what the future holds."

She passed him a bowl filled with dessert and placed one down for herself.

"This looks great, thanks, Valerie."

"Try it and see."

He pushed his spoon into the pie, broke off a portion, and popped it into his mouth. "Mmm, it's delicious."

"Denke."

He was reminded of the pies his mother used to make. They were every bit as good as Valerie's.

"I called around to see Violet. Well, to say goodbye, but I heard she's staying at Lily's."

"Oh, I didn't know."

He nodded.

"You can't leave without saying goodbye to her."

He studied her expression to see whether Violet might have said something to her about him. "I know. I wouldn't do that."

"What time do you start work in the morning?"

"Around nine. Why?"

"I happen to know that Violet gets to the markets way before that. Perhaps you could catch her there." A smile turned up the corners of her lips.

"Yeah, I'll do that." He started on the fruit salad. "Thanks again for everything you've done, Valerie. I don't know what I would've done without having you organize everything for me." He rubbed his forehead.

"I didn't do much."

"Yes, you did. It would've been easier if I'd had a brother or a sister, or someone to help. I should've been able to handle things by myself at my age, but I lost it."

"I understand."

"I couldn't believe she was gone and before I got my head around it, there were all these decisions to make. I knew she wanted an Amish funeral, of course, but not being in the community, it was hard to organize everything."

Valerie said, "Everyone needs help at a time like that."

"You took a load off my shoulders. I'll never forget what you did, and you thought of all the little things the day of the funeral, like having Ed Bontrager collect me and take me to the bishop's house."

"I was happy to do it. I'm used to organizing things."

"I'm not." He continued enjoying his dessert.

"You're always welcome back, you know. If you decide to return."

"Thanks. You and a few others have made me feel like I'd like to return, but it's a huge decision to make and this isn't the best time to do it, while I'm upset about my mother."

"You're right. You need to have a good think about it."

After they finished dessert, they had coffee and talked for a little longer.

The next morning, Nathan was getting dressed when his cell phone rang. It was one of his housemates, Ben. He told Nathan that Abe had given notice. Abe had gotten a job elsewhere and he had to move.

"We'll have to advertise the room if we can't find anyone we know, otherwise, we'll have to chip in for more rent."

"I know," Ben replied. "I'm just giving you a heads up. I wasn't sure when you'd be back."

"Yeah, thanks, neither was I. I've decided I'm coming back now, anyway. I'll clean up here tonight and then I'll be home late tonight."

"Okay, I'll see you then. How did the funeral go?"

"It went well. Pretty much how I expected."

"Sorry I didn't go, but you know how I feel around those people."

"Yeah, I know. It's okay."

When Nathan ended the conversation, it struck him that it was odd to be paying rent somewhere when he could be living in his family home. And if he didn't live there, he could lease it to someone and at least then he would be getting money for it. It would pay his lease in town and then have some leftover.

He had to figure out what to do with his life and figure it out fast. He didn't want to leave his family home vacant and now there was the problem of one of his housemates moving out. Was that a sign? Sign or not, he knew he had to get some kind of direction. If Violet was seriously interested in him, that could be his deciding point that could tip him over to return to the community. If she wasn't, then he'd have to have another good think about everything.

Glancing at the clock on the mantle, he figured if he hurried he'd have enough time to see Violet at the markets before he started work. He wouldn't mention he was going to her Uncle Hezekiah's birthday dinner. Maybe if she thought he was leaving and she wouldn't see him again, that would prompt her to reveal any feelings she had for him.

After Violet had finished her morning delivery, she was wheeling the empty trolley back to the wagon when she got a surprise. Nathan was walking toward her. The markets weren't open for business because it was still too early. *Has he come here to see me?* He looked directly at her and when he came closer, he smiled and gave her a wave. He stopped when she was a few yards away and she was left to close the distance between them with a few more cautious steps. She was relieved when he spoke first.

"Hello, Violet."

"Hi. What brings you here?" If she'd known she'd be seeing him that day, she would've worn a nicer dress and one of her newly sewn prayer *kapps*.

"You do. You bring me here." He chuckled, which made her relax slightly. She was about to say something when he spoke again. "I was hoping to catch you before I leave."

"Where are you going?" The last thing she wanted to hear was that he was going somewhere.

He rubbed his neck. "I'm not sure in the long term, but right now I'm heading back to my old life. One of the guys has moved out of the house and fairly soon we'll have to find someone else to take his place."

She knew he was living with a couple of Amish men who either left the Amish completely or were still on their *rumspringa*. She wasn't totally certain which. "Why would you want to live in a place with other people when you can have one all to yourself? Why not stay at your *mudder's haus?"* She knew now that she'd been wrong to think he cared for her, and she felt foolish. He probably liked her as a friend, but nothing else if he could leave so easily. She had hoped that being amongst the Amish again he would realize that's where he belonged.

"I told you how I feel about being back here."

"I know, but you don't live that far away. Couldn't you live in your *haus* at least, and travel to work every day from there?" Her desire for him to move back to his house was so she could see more of him, since she lived fairly close and if he lived closer to the community, he'd be more inclined to see what he was missing out on.

"You know what I mean. It kind of wouldn't be the same. I'm in a routine where I live and it's not nice being in the house with my mother gone."

Violet nodded and tried her best to hide how disappointed she was. "Are you going for good and leaving the house empty?"

"I don't know what I'm doing with the house yet. I'll most likely sell it. That might be the best thing to do."

"Really?" Violet's stomach churned. Selling the house was so final, and that meant that she might never see him again.

"Yes. I might as well. Maybe I'll buy another house one day. Anyway, I didn't want to leave without saying goodbye. You've been nice to me and I wanted you to know that I appreciate it. You and Valerie have given me a lot of emotional support, especially the day of the funeral. That's when I needed it. I said goodbye to Valerie last night and I stopped by your *haus* on the way back and they said you weren't there."

Violet gasped. "Who did you talk to at my place?"

"Your mother."

Now Violet was annoyed. Her mother could've easily told him she was at Lily's. She visualized exactly how it all played out. She could imagine her mother's steely, determined face when Nathan stood at the door of her home and asked where she was. "What did she say?"

"I asked for a quick word with you and she said you weren't there."

"Did she say where I was?"

He shook his head. "No. That's all she said."

"Oh. Did she ask you inside at least?"

He chuckled. "No. It was your sister. When I was leaving, she ran after me and told me I could find you at Lily's."

"She did? How did that happen?"

"Just as I was leaving, she opened the front door and ran after me. Then before she was called back, she told me you were staying at Lily's and then she said you'd be at the flower markets early this morning."

Violet smiled, picturing her sister doing that good deed, risking a huge punishment from their parents. *Denke, Willow.*

"I don't think your mother likes me, or your father for that matter. Willow was pulled inside and the door was closed." He shook his head.

"Don't take it personally. He's just concerned that I

don't spend too much time with people who aren't in the community. To him, you're an outsider. He's only being protective."

"I know. I will be like that when I'm a father—overprotective."

"I'm glad you came to say goodbye. You'll be missed."

He gave a little laugh as though he doubted that he would be. "Would you be able to do one thing for me, Violet?"

"Sure. What is it?"

"Could you tell your Aunt Nancy that I won't be able to make it to your *onkel's* birthday?"

Her mouth fell open in surprise that he'd been invited, considering what her parents thought of him, and she knew that Aunt Nancy would've discussed the guest list with her *mudder*. She gave a cough, hoping it would cover her instant reaction. "I'll tell her. She'll be disappointed. We'll all be sad you're not staying."

They stared at each other for a moment before he spoke. "Goodbye, Violet."

In that moment, Violet felt a spark between them. Could he feel it too? "Couldn't you wait another few days, at least until after my *Onkel* Hezekiah's birthday?"

He smiled at her. "Once I make up my mind about something, I don't rest until I follow through with it."

If he truly liked her, he'd move heaven and earth to be with her. She wasn't going to push him. "I understand. You'll be welcome if you ever come back. And I hope you come back one day soon."

"Denke, Violet. I tell you what..."

"Jah?" She held her breath and felt her heart pumping hard.

"I will think about it over the next few weeks. I'm at

a point in my life that I need to make some decisions. I've been drifting ever since my father died and now that my mother's gone, it's time I made some kind of a life for myself, somewhere, somehow."

Violet nodded. "I know what you mean."

He chuckled. "I'm not even sure *I* know what I mean. I just need to know where I'm going in life. I don't even know why you've been so nice to me. I can't be appealing as a man since you've seen my weak side. A woman like you should be friends with a solid, dependable man who knows where life is going to take him—knows what he wants."

"You'll figure it out."

He pressed his lips together and nodded while he looked down at the trolley she'd been pushing. "Where are you taking this?"

"Over to the Walkers' wagon." She nodded her head in the direction of the wagon in the distance.

He moved forward and took hold of it. "I'll help you."

"Denke."

Together, they headed out of the farmers market and over to where the wagon was parked in silence. Once he had pushed the trolley up the ramp of the wagon and secured it in the back, he shut the back door and bolted it. "There, all done."

"Denke, Nathan. I'll miss you."

"Will you?" He smiled at her.

"Very much." She had to let him know she liked him without saying it in so many words.

"I might be back. I will make some decisions soon. Bye, Violet."

"Bye, Nathan."

He turned to leave and she watched him walk away.

She wondered if that was the man she was going to marry. Perhaps God had His hand on him and He'd bring him back to her. That was certainly what she hoped, and what she prayed for. At least she knew that he cared for her in some way since he'd taken the time to find her just now.

Chapter Nine

Lily and Violet arrived home late, only half an hour before Elijah came home. They'd bought cooked chickens and all they had to do for the meal was prepare the vegetables and the salads.

Elijah had arrived home not long after they'd started in the kitchen, and minutes after he arrived, they heard Benjamin's buggy drawing up to the house.

After Lily had looked out the window, she said, "He's here already. He can talk to Elijah in the living room until the dinner's ready."

Lily had gone from a giggling girl to a wife who was worried about preparing food for guests. She seemed a different person compared to the one she'd been before she'd gotten married. Violet wondered how her personality might change if she too got married.

"This isn't a set-up, is it?" Violet whispered to Lily.

Lily stopped what she was doing and looked over at Violet. *"Nee,* not at all. I'm not my *mudder."*

The girls giggled.

"That's a relief," Violet said.

Lily tipped her head to the side. "Although, he'd make a good husband."

Violet slapped her lightly on her arm. "Don't start."

"Okay. I'll behave." She lowered her voice. "He's handsome, don't you think?"

"Jah, he is. But I'm looking for more than that in a man."

"Violet, that's not what I meant. Of course you'd need more than that, but at the same time it doesn't hurt to have a man who's nice both on the inside and the outside. It'll give you something nice to look at and make you happy."

"It's good to be happy. Everyone wants that." Looks had never been important to Violet. It was what was inside that counted most. Although having a handsome man wasn't a bad thing.

When they'd all taken seats around the dinner table, they said their silent prayers of thanks for the food. Benjamin's gaze swept across the food as soon as he opened his eyes and as he did so, Violet studied him. His skin was tanned and his eyes were a shade of deep hazel, which complemented his olive skin tone perfectly. When he looked over at her, he smiled, revealing his straight white teeth.

"This all looks *wunderbaar,"* Benjamin said, looking from Violet to Lily.

"Try the chicken. It's Lily's special recipe," Elijah said with a grin.

Violet held in her laughter, figuring Lily must often buy the cooked chickens when she was working late. Elijah didn't seem to mind his working wife taking shortcuts with meals.

They all helped themselves to the food in the center of the table.

"How are you liking it here?" Violet asked Benjamin.

"It's so good that I've decided to stay on."

Violet nodded. "Oh, really?"

He chuckled. "Yeah. I hear your *onkel's* having a big birthday dinner, Violet. I suppose you're going?"

"Jah, are you?"

He nodded before he popped a forkful of chicken in his mouth.

Benjamin was the kind of man that her parents would like to see her with—someone who had strong family ties to the Amish community, who was hardworking, and who was strong and dependable. He'd never put a step wrong and had never left the community.

"I heard that Nathan Beiler hasn't stayed on with us," Elijah said, mainly to Benjamin.

"Has he left? I thought he'd only just returned," Benjamin replied.

"Do you know him, Benjamin?" Violet asked.

"I met him at the funeral. His *mudder's* funeral, just the other day."

Violet nodded. "He might come back."

"You seem particularly close to him, Violet," Elijah said.

"He was a friend, ever since *schul*—still is, I suppose."

"He'll find his way," Benjamin said.

There was no judgment in Benjamin's comment, and Violet liked that.

"Still, it's a shame he's gone. We need more people in the community, especially young people. Now, who wants dessert?" Lily asked.

"I do," Elijah said.

"Me too," Benjamin added.

"I guess that's all of us."

Violet helped Lily remove the plates and bowls from the meal, and then she helped with the dessert of fruit salad with cream and ice-cream. There was also apple pie that Lily had bought from the markets. Working five and a half days a week, it was nearly impossible to have a clean house, do all the washing, and cook all the meals from scratch. Something had to give, and for Lily, it had been the cooking. It didn't hurt to buy a thing or two from the markets.

Violet sat down again just as Lily put the last of the dessert plates on the table.

"I don't know how you manage to do all this and work at the flower stall as well, Lily," Benjamin said.

"She's amazing. It's true," Elijah said before Lily could respond.

Lily gave an embarrassed giggle instead of giving a reply.

"You work too, don't you, Violet?" Benjamin asked.

"Only three days a week, mostly, and more when they need me. I deliver the flowers from where they're grown to the markets. Some of the flowers are flown in, if they're out of season, but most are grown locally right next door to Hezekiah and Nancy's *haus."*

He nodded, appearing not very interested in the details.

"Here, have some apple pie." Elijah stood and cut a slice of pie for Benjamin. "Anyone else?" he asked.

"I'll have a small piece," Violet said.

Elijah sat down after he'd served the pie, taking a sizable piece for himself.

When dinner was over, Lily and Violet washed the

dishes in the kitchen while Elijah and Benjamin sat out in the living room.

When they were halfway through the washing up, Elijah stuck his head around the kitchen door. "How about making us *kaffe,* Lily?"

"Sure, coming right up," Lily said. When she'd made up the tray with the coffee items, she gave the tray to Violet. "You take this out and stay with them. It won't take me long to finish up in here."

"Are you sure?"

"Of course. I'll be out soon." She made shooing motions with her hands, so Violet took the tray to the men in the living room.

"Here you are," Violet said as she placed the coffee tray down on the low table between the two couches that faced each other. After she poured the coffee into two of the cups, she let each man help himself to the sugar and the milk.

"You're not having one, Violet?" Benjamin asked.

"Nee, I've got to get up early tomorrow and *kaffe* keeps me awake. I only drink it in the mornings."

"You're not working all day tomorrow, are you?" Elijah asked.

"Same as usual. A few hours in the morning and then there's nothing to do until the evening."

"Gut! You'd have time in between to show Benjamin around."

Violet was embarrassed and couldn't even look at Benjamin. "Oh, I think Benjamin has been here long enough to know where everything is."

Benjamin chuckled. "I'm working tomorrow, too, Elijah."

Elijah said to Benjamin, "I happen to know you've got time off in the middle of the day."

Violet glanced over at Benjamin and he gave a weak smile. "What do you say, Violet? Would you like to show me around?"

Frowning, Violet looked back at Elijah, annoyed with him. She no more wanted to show Benjamin around than he appeared to want to be shown around. "Um, sure, if Lily doesn't mind me borrowing the buggy again."

Lily walked into the room. "Yeah, you can borrow the buggy. I said you can use it anytime."

"Denke. I'm showing Benjamin around tomorrow."

Lily sat down next to Elijah. "That's a *gut* idea. Where are you going?"

"I don't know." Violet looked over at Benjamin. "What kind of things are you interested in?"

He pulled his mouth to one side. "I guess I'd just like to see what's around the area."

Violet smiled and was grateful he was so polite.

"Good. That's settled," Elijah said, looking pleased with himself.

When it got later into the evening, Elijah and Lily went into the kitchen and left Benjamin and Violet alone.

Violet leaned over and whispered, "It's okay if you don't want to look around tomorrow."

"I'd like to. Why? Don't you want to?"

"Oh, I don't mind. I thought you might have only said so to be polite. It's not necessary."

He studied her with wide eyes. "You're a mystery to me, Violet."

She stifled the laughter that she felt bubbling up from within. "Me?"

"Jah. I'd like to spend some time with you tomorrow. It's not so much that I want to see the sights."

Violet was taken aback. He actually liked her. This big, strong, handsome man actually liked her. She felt her cheeks warm and had to look away from him.

"Are we still on for tomorrow? We can take my buggy and I can collect you from wherever you'll be."

Nodding, Violet said, "Okay. I'll be back here by about eleven o'clock. Would that suit?"

"I can be here by twelve."

"Good." As soon as she agreed, with perfect timing, Elijah and Lily came out of the kitchen.

Benjamin sprang to his feet, thanked Lily for the dinner, and said goodbye to everyone.

After Benjamin had gone, Elijah went up to bed, which left Lily and Violet alone. Lily pulled Violet down onto the couch beside her.

"Well, what do you think of him?"

"He's lovely. He's really nice."

"I think he's perfect for you and he's someone you don't have to worry about."

Violet didn't ask but she guessed she was referring to Nathan as being someone she *did* have to worry about. Nathan seemed a little lost, and that made Benjamin a far better-looking choice for her. And besides, she was still flattered that someone as handsome as he would find her appealing.

Violet had lost so much confidence in herself since she started wearing glasses even though Willow had told her they made her look more interesting. It didn't matter what her younger sister thought; Violet was far more concerned about what people outside her family thought of her appearance. She wasn't vain by any means, but she didn't want to look so unappealing that people recoiled away in horror, and that's how bad she felt she looked.

Chapter Ten

Violet waited on the porch for Benjamin to collect her since it was just coming up on midday. While she waited, her thoughts turned to Nathan. Many scenarios ran through her head of what he was doing and where he was. Surely if Nathan liked her as a girlfriend or his future wife, he would've stayed around a bit longer. Besides, was it really a good idea to walk out and leave his house vacant, not knowing what he was going to do with it?

She thought about the future and what kind of life she might have if she married Nathan. He was troubled, and that would make for an unstable relationship. Benjamin, on the other hand, was the opposite—he knew what he wanted in life. And what's more, Benjamin didn't have a girlfriend. He couldn't have had one or he wouldn't have agreed for her to show him around.

She looked up when she heard hoofbeats, and saw Benjamin's buggy heading toward the house. Pushing her glasses further up her nose, she stepped down from the porch. Seeing that he was staring at her, she got nervous and tugged her black shawl tighter around her shoulders and then stood fiddling with the ends of the shawl while the buggy drew up beside her.

Once they'd exchanged greetings, she stepped into the buggy.

"Nice day," he said, looking up at the sky for an instant.

"Jah, it is. There's just enough of a cool breeze to stop it from being too hot."

"You look like you're cold with your shawl wrapped around you." He turned the buggy to take it back down the driveway.

"I think it'll get colder. Someone at the markets said rain's expected this afternoon."

"There's no sign of it yet. I'll get you back home before the rain hits. We've both got to get back to work."

When he glanced over at her, she nodded and gave him a small smile. "How much time do you have? I don't have to be back at the markets until four, so I have to be back at the *haus* around three."

"I've got a whole two hours," he said. "Where do you suggest we go?"

"I'll direct you. I'll show you around the back roads and around the farms. Unless you'd like to see the covered bridges? They're very pretty."

"Nee, I've seen enough bridges. I know the ones you mean, and they're beautiful, but I've seen them before."

"Okay, take a left up here." She took him along the roads where the best views of the county were.

"That's Valerie's *haus* over there and then that big patch of green behind it is the Pattersons' land."

After they'd been driving for several minutes, Benjamin said, "Shall we stop and take a walk?"

"Okay."

He pulled the buggy off the road and secured his horse. The road they were on wasn't sealed; it was a dirt road that created too much dust when cars went past. Thankfully, very few cars traveled on these lonely back roads that only led to properties of Amish folk, and the roads didn't link to any major roads.

"Where would you like to walk? We could go back that way, or up here." Violet stood at the edge of the road with her hands clutching the ends of her shawl like some kind of a security blanket. She was more than a little flattered that Benjamin might be interested in her.

"There seems to be a track along the fence line here." He set off walking with long strides, and Violet hurried to catch up.

"What's it like where you've come from?" Violet asked.

"The community is much smaller. There are only four families."

"That is really small!"

"The countryside is pretty similar to here. We have a lot of visitors from your community, or we have had over the past years."

"*Jah,* I think I read something in one of the newspapers." The Amish newspapers always gave information on who was traveling to where and whom they'd stayed with. "You must like it here if you're staying on."

He slowed down a little, allowing her to walk alongside. "There are more opportunities here."

"For work?"

"*Jah,* and for meeting people."

He glanced over at her and she looked away, embarrassed once more. It was obvious that he'd moved here to find a wife as well as for employment.

"Tell me some more about yourself, Violet. Is it only you and Willow in your *familye* or do you have other siblings?"

"It's just me and Willow. I'm the oldest." As soon as she said that, she had to wonder why she had stated the obvious. It seemed a silly thing to say. "And what about you?"

"I have two older *schweschdere* and five older *brieder,* and I'm the youngest."

"And have they all stayed on in the community?"

"My two older *schweschdere* have, but my *brieder* moved away to different communities." After a pause, he asked, "What kind of things do you like to do?"

There was something about answering all these questions that didn't feel natural to her. It felt like he was questioning her to see if she measured up to his expectations in a girlfriend, and a future wife. "I like to sew and I like to cook." Those were the things that she thought he wanted to hear, but also things that all the women she knew could do.

"That's it? No weird hobbies? You don't own any strange pets, or have a habit of collecting things?"

Violet giggled. "No to the pets, and no, I don't collect anything. What would I collect, anyway?"

"I don't know." He stooped down, picked something up off the ground and handed it to her. "Triangular rocks maybe?"

She looked at the rock in her hand and laughed when she saw it was triangular. "I don't remember that I've ever seen a stone this shape before. This can be the first one in my collection. I wonder how it was formed."

He chuckled. "We'll find a creek and see if we can skip that rock along the water."

"Not with this rock. It's special and I'm keeping it. You'll have to get another rock to do that."

"Flat rocks are better anyway."

"You won't find a creek around here unless we walk about another hour in that direction," she said, pointing to the north of them. "And we don't have the time today."

He stopped and glanced back at the buggy. "We will if we take the buggy."

Violet raised her eyebrows. "Do you want to go to the creek?"

"*Jah,* come on." He turned around and headed back to the buggy, and Violet had to hurry again to keep up with his long strides.

Chapter Eleven

Once Violet and Benjamin were back in the buggy, Violet showed him the shortcut to take. The road became more narrow and rougher the closer they got to the water.

Benjamin was nice; Violet admitted that much to herself. Elijah seemed like he was the one keen for them to spend time together, but Violet suspected her Aunt Nancy was somehow involved.

Minutes later, they arrived. Once they were on foot, Violet pointed to the water and then followed Benjamin as he went first along the trail. The only choice was to walk single file. When they came closer to the river, the path widened and he slowed until she was beside him.

"Ah, here we are." He stared at the water and then looked down around his feet. "But there aren't many stones. No good ones."

"Nee, and you can't have my triangle stone because I left it in the buggy."

"Okay. How about we walk up this way?"

As they walked on, the conversation flowed more freely. He talked a little about what he wanted to achieve by coming to her community and how he wanted to build a house. He'd been offered land by a member of the community and he wanted to save enough money to start his building project.

What he was talking about was interesting and Violet wished she had something just as remarkable to tell him about herself and her plans for the future.

"You're very brave for leaving your family and coming all this way to start a new life here."

"Nee, I'm not that brave. I knew a lot of people from here. I knew Elijah before I moved here, and of course, I know Bruno."

"I'd never move away from here—away from my family."

"You'd have no reason to move away."

Violet shook her head. "I'd never want to."

He glanced up at the sky. "Still no sign of that rain you were talking about. But still, maybe we should start heading back. I'd hate to be late getting back to work."

"Okay."

He walked ahead of her, and then he turned around. "I've enjoyed this. I never would've thought to do something in the middle of the day like this. Normally I would've waited for a day off. I was reluctant to do this when Elijah suggested it. I hope you didn't think my reluctance had anything to do with you and not wanting to spend time with you."

"Nee," she said to be polite, but knew it was about her glasses and her being a plain girl. He could've been spending time with a much prettier girl if he'd wanted to. *"Jah.* It's amazing how much you can do in a short space of time like this. I've gotten used to it with my workday always being divided."

When they got back into the buggy, Violet picked up her stone from the floor of the buggy and held it in her hand.

Benjamin saw what she'd done and smiled. "You're serious about that collection?"

"I might be. It's such an unusual stone."

"One of a kind, I'd reckon." When they were halfway back to the *haus,* Benjamin asked, "Can I see you again, Violet?"

"Jah, there's *Onkel* Hezekiah's birthday on Thursday. Are you going to that?"

"I am, but I mean besides that? Maybe on Saturday afternoon we could do something together if you're not busy?"

Violet was flattered, but she still didn't feel the same way about him that she felt about Nathan. She had to remind herself that Nathan wasn't there and was probably never coming back. If God was presenting her with a good man, should she turn her back and pin all her hopes on Nathan?

"Okay, that would be nice," she said, feeling too embarrassed and awkward to say no even if she'd wanted to.

When Benjamin dropped her back at Lily's house, she hurried inside to look at the clock in the kitchen. She saw she had a few minutes to spare before she had to leave to head back to the markets.

Violet secured her buggy and hurried into the markets. It was then that she saw Aunt Nancy talking to Lily.

When she got closer, Lily glanced up at her and Nancy spun around to face her. "There you are, Violet. Hello. I hear you spent a good part of the day with Benjamin."

Violet grimaced and looked over at Lily. "News travels fast." Couldn't Lily have kept that to herself?

"Jah, news like that certainly does; your *mudder* will be pleased."

It wasn't a good idea for her mother to find out as well. She'd be planning the wedding in no time. She frowned at her aunt. "What does *Mamm* have to do with this?"

Nancy shook her head and patted Violet on her shoulder in a comforting manner. "Forget I said anything."

"How was your time with Benjamin? Did you enjoy yourself?" Lily asked.

Violet nodded. *"Jah,* it was okay."

"Well, I'll leave you girls to it. I just stopped by the markets to pick up a few things." Nancy lifted her bag of groceries higher.

When she'd gone, Violet continued to load the trolley with the flowers that needed to go back to the Walkers' place. It was a job that one of the Walkers' sons used to do, but now they were doing more important things with expanding their business into other regions.

"Don't be mad with me. I've got no control over my *mudder,"* Lily said.

"I'm not mad at you, but I just sometimes wish people would just let things be."

"And by 'things' you mean you?"

Violet nodded. "Exactly. Why does everyone take such an interest in everything I do? I just wish I was invisible sometimes."

"Just tell me—what did you like about him?"

"He's very nice." Violet said in a small voice, not being able to verbalize what she liked about him. She wasn't about to tell Lily she didn't like him as much as Nathan, because she was trying her best to forget him.

Maybe Benjamin would grow on her if she spent more time with him. She was prepared to give him a chance.

"I knew you'd like him; he's lovely."

"Denke for inviting him to dinner last night."

"It wasn't me. It was Elijah who invited him. I thought I said that. Anyway, I'm glad things worked out. It would've been awkward if you hadn't gotten along with him."

"He's asked me out again."

Lily's eyebrows flew up so high they nearly touched her prayer *kapp.* "Oh, that's good! I'm glad."

"Don't look so surprised."

"Well, I am."

"Wasn't that your plan?"

Lily giggled. "I'm not saying a word. My lips are sealed." Lily put her fingertips to her mouth and made the motion of zipping her lips.

Nathan had thought long and hard about his life. Being with some of the people in the community, like Valerie and Violet and even old Mrs. Gingerich, had touched his heart. Deep down, he knew where he belonged. The world was a harsh place. He'd found his way in it, but it might be time to return to the community. That's what his mother would've wanted and he had to think where he was going to spend eternity. He wanted to be with his mother again one day. As the bishop had told him, this life was so temporary—like a vapor. Eternity was forever.

If he came back, he'd hope to marry Violet if she'd have him. He guessed she liked him a little and he would be free to express his feelings for her. The first step in the process was to go to Violet's Uncle Hezekiah's birthday. It touched him deeply that he'd been invited. It was like a sign that people would wholeheartedly accept him back into the community and then it would be as though he'd never left. He'd get baptized and be a proper member, and then he'd get married and have a family.

The night of Hezekiah's birthday, he was back at his mother's house. He'd stopped by Ed Bontrager's house and asked if he could travel with him to the birthday dinner. Without hesitation, Ed agreed and offered to collect him from his mother's house and Nathan accepted his offer. He knew that would be better than arriving at Nancy and Hezekiah's house in a car and that way he wouldn't feel so out of place.

It made sense to stay at his mother's house that night. He'd arrived in his work clothes and then discovered he didn't have any suitable clothes with him. Planning wasn't a strong point of his and he knew that was one of the things he'd have to change if he was ever to gain control over his life. He had to grow up. It affected him that he hadn't been able to fully organize his mother's funeral. Now he had no mother and no relatives and that meant he only had himself to rely on. In that moment, he closed his eyes and prayed for God to give him strength and help him to be a better man.

If he drove back home for clothes, it'd make him late and he didn't want Ed to be hanging around waiting. He looked in his room and found the white shirt he'd worn for the funeral and then he found an old pair of jeans. *That'll have to do.* He knew he was taking a risk going to the party. He was almost certain he'd face people who didn't approve of him, but he'd rely on God to make it through.

Chapter Twelve

When Violet arrived at her uncle's birthday dinner on the following Thursday night, Valerie met her just as she was getting out of Elijah and Lily's buggy. "Can I speak with you for a moment, Violet?" Valerie nodded and smiled at Lily, and then at Elijah when he came around the side of the buggy.

"Okay." Violet glanced over at Lily, who was now beside her.

"We'll go inside, Violet," Lily said as she started walking forward.

Elijah and Lily went into the house, and Violet was keen to know why Valerie was looking so concerned.

"What is it?" Violet inquired as Valerie stepped closer.

"It's nothing to worry about. I've come outside to let you know that there is someone inside who we didn't think was coming."

"Nathan?"

Valerie nodded. *"Jah."*

Violet was pleased but then immediately thought of Benjamin, who she'd been out with. Her worlds were colliding. It wasn't good. She was angry with herself for not waiting for Nathan. "Is he back to stay?"

"*Jah,* he says he is."

Violet put her hand over her heart. She was so pleased. "That's *wunderbaar!*"

Valerie put her arm around Violet. "Best you talk to him and see what you can find out."

"*Jah,* of course I'll talk to him. I'm surprised he's here with so many people."

"Your aunt must've invited everyone she knew."

"The whole community and then some."

Valerie laughed and then said, "I've got a few people to see."

"You go ahead. I'll talk to Nathan."

Valerie walked off to greet other people, leaving Violet still in shock that Nathan was there. Looking down at her dress, she was glad that she'd worn one of her better ones. She pinched her cheeks to give them some color and was glad that she'd added some rosemary and lavender to the rinsing water when she'd washed her hair earlier that day. Taking a deep breath, she smoothed down her dress and straightened her prayer *kapp.* When Violet walked into the house, she saw Nathan almost immediately. His eyes and face lighted up and he gave her a wave as he moved toward her.

"Hello, Violet."

"I didn't expect to see you here. I thought you'd left." She looked down at the clothes he was wearing. He wasn't in Amish clothing, but he looked good, in his white shirt that showed off his tanned skin, and his faded jeans. "Is it true that you're here to stay?"

"It depends on you."

She swallowed hard. "Me?"

He nodded.

What was he talking about? How could him coming back to the community depend on her? It was his choice whether he came back or not. She couldn't make that important life-changing decision for him. "I'm not sure what you mean."

He looked around him at the crowd. "Can we go somewhere to talk?"

Violet looked around too. "I guess we could go outside."

He nodded and together they walked out the front door.

She suggested, "Why don't we walk around the side of the house and that way we don't have to greet people as they come to the house?"

"That's a good idea." Once they were by themselves, Nathan said, "Violet, I haven't been able to stop thinking about you since I left."

She turned to face him directly and desperately wanted to say that she felt the same about him, but she kept quiet and let him continue.

"I've had a long hard think about everything. About my life and what it would be like if I stayed in the community and what it would be like if I left for good." He rubbed his clean-shaven chin.

"And?"

"I know I'd come back to the community if you…if you and I could…"

Violet frowned. She wanted to be his girlfriend if he came back, but he had to understand a few things. This wasn't right. "Nathan, you can't come back to the community for me or anybody else. It has to be for you."

"It would be for me, Violet. I'd be coming back for myself."

Violet pushed her glasses further up her nose. "It sounds like you're making it conditional upon something else."

"I thought this through, long and hard."

"I just don't want you to make a mistake, or a decision that you could regret later on." As much as she liked him, she had to be with a man who was stable. Not a man who was in and out of the community. She knew if he made that decision for himself he was reliable enough to stay, but not if he made that decision dependent upon something else.

He shook his head. "I don't see that I would regret it."

"Have you spoken to the bishop?"

"I've spoken to the bishop in the way that we had a general conversation about things. I was going to speak to the bishop after we spoke. Don't you want me to come back? Are you judging me by my unstable father? Violet, I'm nothing like him."

"Nee, I'm not judging you by anyone."

"Why are you like this, then?"

Violet had to be truthful. "I've thought of little else but you since you left. I'm just concerned that you won't be making the decision about *Gott* and returning to the community from your heart."

He had his mouth open to speak when someone appeared beside them from around the corner of the house. It was Benjamin, and from the angry look on his face, he'd overheard everything.

"Nathan, why have you pulled Violet away to speak to her like this—alone?"

Nathan shook his head, looked down at the ground, and then looked back at Benjamin. "I was having a quiet private word with my friend."

"It's not right for two unmarried people to be alone like this." Benjamin then looked at Violet. "I should tell your *vadder,* Violet."

Violet frowned. "I don't mean to be rude, Benjamin, but this has nothing to do with you. We're just talking. We're not doing anything wrong."

"I heard your whole conversation, Nathan. You're making coming back to the community dependent upon Violet having some romantic notions about you and that's wrong. If you come back, you should come back because you want to walk with *Gott.* You should examine your heart—and your mind."

Nathan breathed out heavily and looked straight ahead. "I guess I've just made a fool of myself."

"You haven't made a fool of yourself," Violet insisted.

"I'm sorry to have bothered you, Violet. I'll get out of everybody's way."

"Don't go, Nathan." She stepped toward Nathan and reached for his arm, but Benjamin grabbed her hand before it reached him.

"Let him go, Violet," Benjamin ordered.

By the time he finished speaking, Nathan had gone. Violet pulled her arm away from Benjamin and walked around the corner to see where Nathan was. She hurried after him. "Nathan, stop!"

He stopped in his tracks, turned around, and waited until she caught up. "Everything he said is right, Violet. I made a mistake in coming here. I'm not meant to come back. The signs are clear. Is Benjamin your boyfriend now?"

"Nee, of course not. He isn't."

"He seems to think he's your boyfriend, or more like

your *vadder* the way he's ordering you around." Nathan stared back at the house.

Violet glanced behind her to see what Nathan was staring at. It was Benjamin, who was glaring at them with his arms folded.

"He's probably a better man for you than I am."

"Don't say that, Nathan. He's not!"

"I need to think and pray about everything a whole lot more." He turned and walked away.

"Where are you going?" she called after him.

"Back to my house. Please tell Ed I've already gone."

"Are you walking there? It'll take a long time if you are."

"Time is something I've got a lot of, and besides it will help clear my head. Just tell Ed, please. He was driving me home. I came here with him."

"I can drive you there in the buggy."

"Stay here, Violet." He gave her a wave and kept walking.

Benjamin grabbed her arm. "Violet."

She pulled her arm out of his grasp and glared at him. She'd never be involved with a man like Benjamin, and now Nathan had been driven away for good. It was people like Benjamin with no compassion who had driven Nathan away in the first place.

"I need a moment alone, Benjamin."

Benjamin stared at her before he slowly turned and walked back into the house.

Violet walked back and forth behind the house, too upset to talk to anyone. She just wanted to go home. Why were people so mean sometimes? The Word of God talked about standing in a sinner's way; weren't all these mean Amish people standing in Nathan's way?

And why couldn't they see that—all these holier-than-thou people? She shook her head and groaned loudly when she realized she was being just as judgmental about them.

All she wanted was for Nathan to feel comfortable enough to return. He was a sensitive man. If only he was more thick-skinned, he might be able to let people's words slide right off him. Instead, he took things to heart. She thought about the hurt and dismay in his eyes when Benjamin had said those things to him. Should she have stood up for him more and walked after him when he left?

If only Benjamin hadn't followed them out of the house. Benjamin must've been lurking around the corner, listening in on their conversation. Violet closed her eyes and prayed for Nathan. She wanted him to return to the community, but maybe there was another path Nathan had to follow, or maybe *Gott* had more trials for him to go through before he called him back into the fold.

After Violet prayed, peace washed over her like a warm shower of water. After she'd mentally placed Nathan in God's hands, she walked back into the house.

Nathan's first reaction had been to swing a punch at Benjamin, hard enough to knock him out cold. He'd taken boxing lessons to keep him fit, so he could've swung one before Benjamin knew what was happening. Violence never solved anything, but it sure would've made him feel good at the time.

As Nathan walked along the side of the dark road with only a half moon to light the way, he remembered crying as a child, scared of the dark. He was sent to bed in a darkened room and left to imagine scary creatures under the bed. His father would not even allow the bedroom door to be open slightly to let some light in.

He knew if he crept out at night he would face his father's wrath. It was scary to stay in that darkened room, hiding under the quilt. That's when he first learned to pray, and every morning when he woke he thanked God for keeping the monsters away. When he grew older, he realized that the only monster in the house was the alcohol with which his father overindulged.

He wasn't scared of the dark as a grown man; he wasn't scared of anything. Benjamin had made him feel like an idiot, but perhaps he hadn't fully thought things through. Why would he open himself up to the community only to be hurt again? Benjamin didn't even know him and hadn't known his parents and somehow, he was against him.

Then Nathan remembered the people who had been wonderful to him, like Violet, Valerie, Nancy, and Hezekiah.

When he was halfway home and had calmed down some more, he wondered if Violet had been the reason he was thinking of returning. Yes, she was an incentive, but she was right, he couldn't let her be the only reason for coming back. It was kind of hard to take her out of the picture and make a decision. It would be easy to walk away from the community just as he was walking home right now—one foot after the other and never looking back. That is, if it weren't for Violet and if it weren't for one day wanting to see his mother again. In the past, every time he'd thought about returning, someone like Benjamin would block his way.

Right now, he was flip-flopping with his decision

and he hated being indecisive. He remembered a scripture about God not liking people to be lukewarm. He'd rather someone be hot or cold and he would spew the lukewarm out of his mouth. He'd have to make a choice and the sooner the better. Was he going to go back to the community or continue with the life he already had out of the community?

Chapter Thirteen

Violet slowly walked back into her aunt's house and found Benjamin waiting by the door.

"Where's he going?" Benjamin tossed his head back and stared in the direction Nathan had gone.

"Who?"

"Nathan, of course."

She knew who he meant, but she didn't feel like talking about Nathan and she hoped Benjamin sensed her annoyance. "He's walking back home."

"Why? He only just got here."

"He's obviously upset by what you said to him and I don't blame him."

He frowned at her. "It was only the truth. He must've misunderstood a few things, that's all."

"He was coming back to the community, but I don't know what he's going to do now."

He took a step toward her. "Was there something going on between you and Nathan?"

She shook her head. *"Nee,* nothing like that. He said he's got a lot to think about."

Benjamin offered, "Do you think I should go after him and talk to him?"

"I don't think that will help. I think he just needs to be by himself."

Benjamin gestured toward the door. "We should join the others inside. Unless you think I should find Nathan and drive him home."

Violet grabbed him by the arm. *"Nee,* leave him be. I don't think it'll help if you go after him."

He nodded. "If you say so."

"Now I need to find *Onkel* Hezekiah and wish him a happy birthday. And then I have to find Ed Bontrager and tell him Nathan's walked home." She walked inside the house and Benjamin followed.

Willow appeared and said hello to Benjamin.

"Hi, Willow."

Willow lunged forward and grabbed Violet's hand. "Aunt Nancy needs your help in the kitchen urgently. She said to hurry."

Violet glanced up at Benjamin. "Excuse me."

"Go right ahead."

Once they were in the kitchen, Willow blurted out, "Did you hear Nathan is coming back to the community?"

Violet nodded, knowing Willow's news was now old and inaccurate. He'd probably never be back.

"Why are you looking like that? It's true. He's been talking to the bishop and everything. I know it's true. It's not gossip."

Violet sighed. "Just don't talk about him for the moment. Did you just lie about Aunt Nancy wanting to see me?"

"Whoops. I didn't mean to. I had to get you away

from Benjamin so I could tell you the news about Nathan."

Violet frowned at her younger sister.

"Anyway, why don't you want to talk about Nathan?"

"If you must know, I was just speaking to him and one thing after another happened and now I'm not so sure he's coming back." She didn't want to tell her how Benjamin had interfered.

"Isn't that what you wanted, for him to come back? I was only excited for you."

"I like him, but not if he's not going to stay in the community. How do I know he's going to stay for good? He might only come back and stay for a few months and then leave again."

"Violet, anyone can do anything. I think you're being silly and looking at the downside." Violet was shocked at her little sister. Willow continued, "Anyway, you're best off to forget him."

"Will you make up your mind? One minute you want me to be with him and the next, you don't. I can't keep up with the way your mind flip-flops around over him."

"I'll like him if he comes back and stays. Anyway, he makes you crazy. And you're always depressed when he's around. You're not happy. You're nicer to be around since you've been spending time with Benjamin."

"And how would you know that?"

"Because I can see your face when you see Benjamin. Your face lights up."

Violet doubted that was true. "Does it?"

"*Jah.* And now we'll have to help Aunt Nancy because we told Benjamin that's what we were doing."

"I have to find Ed." Violet found Ed and she saw him look disappointed when she said Nathan had walked home. Judging from his face, Ed had guessed Nathan had a falling out with someone.

Throughout the party, Violet could see that her mother and Aunt Nancy were pleased that Benjamin stayed by her side. All the while, Violet's mind was elsewhere. It bothered her that Nathan might have come back except for Benjamin's interference. Surely Nathan would've known he had to come back because of a decision from his heart and mind, and not because of her. She was only making doubly certain he was doing it for himself, but Benjamin overhearing had taken things the wrong way.

When the night was over, Violet went back home with Elijah and Lily. When they walked in the door, she excused herself and went to bed.

She knew Lily would've only wanted to talk about Benjamin and ask why Nathan had suddenly disappeared from the party, and she wasn't up to explaining things that she didn't even fully understand herself.

Violet slowly changed out of her clothes, took off her glasses, and slipped on her nightgown. As she pulled the nightgown over her head, her *kapp* came off and fell to the floor. She stooped down to pick it up and then tossed it on one of the nightstands in readiness for the next day. Normally, she would've brushed out her hair, but tonight she left it in long braids and slipped between the sheets, still not able to get the horrible scene out of her mind.

Anger rose within Violet over Benjamin being the cause of Nathan leaving. He'd had no right to butt into her conversation with Nathan, and what's more, he'd obviously been listening in on what they'd been saying from his spot around the corner. That fact lowered her opinion of him. Who was he to judge Nathan when he was doing the wrong thing in eavesdropping?

She had to wonder whether her heart longed for Nathan only because he was always just out of reach. Was she scared of having a real relationship, or did she feel safe longing for something that would never be?

Chapter Fourteen

Nancy woke up and saw that Hezekiah was not beside her. She knew that she had overslept; she always woke before him and got up to make his breakfast.

"Hezekiah!" she yelled out. When there was no response, she knew that he had left without waking her. At first, she worried about his heart problem. Was he lying ill somewhere within the house, too weak to call out? Then a smiled tugged at the corners of her lips when she remembered he told her to sleep in after such a late night. He'd gotten up and made his own breakfast and judging by the silence in the house, he'd gotten himself to work. Although she liked to see him off with a hearty cooked breakfast, she didn't like doing it after a late night. A late morning was far preferable.

There had been well over two hundred people at the dinner and that had meant a lot of cleaning, cooking, and preparation before, and plenty of work afterward. Today there'd still be loads of work to do with cleaning the *haus* after all the guests.

Nancy lay in bed for a while, soaking up the luxury of those few extra hours of sleep. Her thoughts soon turned to the person for whom the party had really been held, and that was Violet. The birthday dinner had been solely to invite young men who would be suitable for her unmarried niece.

The party had been almost a waste of time because it seemed that Benjamin and Violet were already getting along well, thanks to Elijah inviting him for dinner the week before.

Nathan Beiler presented a problem in the equation. If she had not seen how Violet and Nathan were talking to each other outside the kitchen window right after the party had started, she would've had no concerns. Although she could not hear what was said, she could certainly see how they had looked at one another. She'd only spied on them briefly, not wanting to be discovered. Nancy was sure those two were in love.

Perhaps Violet had said something to him that caused him to leave. Had she let him down gently and told him she didn't have feelings for him? It had puzzled Nancy and had been on her mind the entire evening, all through the party. If Violet had told him with her mouth that she wasn't interested, her eyes had said something quite different. If there was one thing Nancy knew about, that was love. She considered herself an excellent matchmaker. Benjamin was her choice for Violet, but did Violet's heart already reside with another? And was that other man Nathan? What had her niece said that had sent the young man scurrying away from the birthday dinner?

The bigger question was, how could she find out? Recalling that Valerie had done most of the arranging for Nathan's mother's funeral and that she was close to Nathan, she figured Valerie would know a thing or two. Stopping by Valerie's was as good a place as any to start. She would pay Valerie a visit as soon as she got herself dressed and organized for the day.

Nancy pushed open the door of Valerie's house and stuck her head through.

"Yoo-hoo. Valerie? Are you home?"

"Jah, I'm just in the kitchen. Come on through."

She found Valerie in the kitchen, baking. "What on earth are you doing? It looks like quite a project."

"Why is it so unusual that I'm making cookies? Ed and his boys like my cookies and I like to keep a good supply."

"I can see the level of concentration on your face."

"Oh, now, stop it. Sit down and I'll make you a cup of *kaffe."*

"No need. I just had one. I'll help myself to a glass of water." Nancy reached for a glass on the high shelf next to the sink and pulled one down. When she'd filled it with water from the tap, she took a sip and then sat down at the kitchen table with the glass clutched in her hands.

"That was a good dinner last night. I think everyone enjoyed themselves," Valerie said.

"Jah, I hope so, but you know the real reason I had the birthday dinner, don't you?"

"It wasn't to celebrate Hezekiah's fifty-something-or-other birthday?"

Nancy giggled. "Nerida asked me to find a man for Violet. I think you know that, and anyway, by the time the party came around she'd found one by herself." Nancy didn't tell Valerie that she was responsible for that as well.

Valerie's eyes widened as she stared at Nancy. *"Jah,* and I don't think he is the only one who likes her."

Nancy leaned forward. "I'm guessing... Do you mean Nathan?"

"Ah. You noticed, too?"

Nancy leaned into the straight wooden back of the chair with both hands still clasped around the glass in front of her. "They were in deep conversation about something. I saw them outside when I looked out the kitchen window. They were by themselves talking, and then he suddenly left. Do you know what that was about?"

"I don't. She's not about to tell me what happened between the two of them."

"I wasn't thinking of her telling you. I know you're quite close with Nathan."

Valerie laughed. "Not that close." She cut out the cookies while Nancy looked on. Then Valerie placed the tray of cookies in the heated oven and washed her hands. "There. Another chore done for the day." When she sat opposite Nancy, she said, "And anyway, I don't know if you'd say I was close to him at all. I don't think he would tell me what's on his mind, but I would say we're friends on some level. He was grateful I helped out with his *mudder's* funeral. He thanked me several times."

"Are you worried that he just left the party? Have you spoken with him?"

"I haven't had time. I was thinking of calling over to see him on my way through town. When he arrived, he told me he was coming back to the community. Are you thinking he's changed his mind just because he left the dinner early?"

"It's not just that. It was the *way* he left, so suddenly, as though he was upset by something."

Valerie looked at her and raised her eyebrows.

"Why don't we both visit him?" asked Nancy.

"Do you mean today?"

"Why not? Now that I've got no *kinner* left at home, my days are free."

"Okay, but after we call in and see Nathan, do you want to come into town with me?"

"That sounds good. I have a few things I need to collect."

"Can you wait until these cookies bake?" Valerie asked.

Nancy smiled. "I can, but I might need that cup of *kaffe* after all."

Valerie said, "Coming right up."

Valerie went along in Nancy's buggy to visit Nathan. When they got there, they were surprised to see a man hammering a "for sale" sign into the front yard.

Valerie got out of the buggy as soon as Nancy pulled it up and she scurried to the front door. Finding it slightly ajar, she pushed it open and called out for Nathan. Nancy was right behind her, and looked over her shoulder to see Nathan packing things into boxes.

"Nathan, where are you going?" Valerie asked.

He straightened up. "Hello, Valerie. I'm moving back into the house I was living in before."

"I thought you were coming back here to stay in the community?" Nancy asked.

"Plans changed." He scratched his head. "I'm sorry. I should've told you."

Valerie walked over to him. "Let's sit down and talk about things."

He shook his head. "It's no use talking about anything. Things have just never worked out for me in the community. I thought I'd give it another go…" He breathed out heavily. "I always seem to end up disappointed."

Valerie looked over at Nancy, who moved closer, and asked, "Is there anything that we can do? Do you want to speak with the bishop or maybe Hezekiah?" Hezekiah was a deacon and many people found him easier to talk to than the bishop.

"I don't think so. Thank you both for everything you've done. You've been really good to me, helping with the funeral and everything."

"When are you going?" Valerie asked.

"Soon. I'm heading off as soon as I finish packing these few things."

"I wish you didn't have to go," Nancy said.

"You're always welcome back here. You know that, don't you?" Valerie asked.

Nancy could tell Valerie felt motherly toward the young man. Valerie had never had any children of her own, and now this young man had no parents. If he'd stayed on in the community, it might have been good for both of them.

Nancy guessed that him leaving had something to do with Violet, but she didn't like to ask, and besides he probably wouldn't have told her.

"At least let us help you with your packing," Nancy said.

"I'm just about done. The realtor said he'd see that the rest of the things were cleared out. I'm just taking a few keepsakes, and that's all really. If you know of anyone who wants any furniture, they're welcome to come here and take it."

"Are you sure, Nathan?"

"Why don't you leave everything here like this, just for a few months? Your mother has only just gone and you mightn't be thinking clearly about things in your time of grief. I know when my husband died, I thought about selling the farm and moving away from everything, but I stayed and just sold off the land and kept the *haus*. Later, I was glad I stayed where I knew people. My family was putting a lot of pressure on me to move."

He nodded at what Valerie had to say. "I just need to make a clean start of everything."

"I can understand that," Valerie said. "If you come back, you don't need this house anyway."

Nancy added, "You're always welcome to stay with Hezekiah and me if you decide to return. We've got a big house and so many spare bedrooms that we don't know what to do with them."

"Thank you. I'll keep that in mind. That's very kind of you—both of you."

"Do you have our addresses so you can write to us?"

"Forget writing, Valerie. Young people don't do that these days. Stop by and see us sometime. Don't be a stranger, Nathan."

"I will. I mean, I won't." He chuckled. "I will stop by and visit both of you."

"That would be good." Nancy stepped forward and gave him a quick hug, and Valerie did the same.

"We don't want you to go, but we'll leave you to it if we can't talk you out of it," Valerie said.

They walked to the door and he followed close behind them. When they reached the buggy, they looked back at Nathan, who was standing in the doorway.

Nancy whispered, "Look at him, Valerie. He's like

a lost soul, a lost little boy. I just want to put my arms around him and hold him tight."

Valerie looked back at him and then stepped into the buggy. "There's nothing we can do, Nancy. He wants to leave and there's nothing we can do about it. We can pray for him and leave him in *Gott's* hands."

"*Jah,* that's exactly what we'll do." Nancy instructed the horse to move forward and they waved to Nathan as they drove away.

As the buggy made its way into town, Nancy's thoughts drifted to her niece. She was glad now that Violet had Benjamin to occupy her, and hopefully, in time, she would forget about whatever feelings she'd had for Nathan.

Chapter Fifteen

News in the Amish community travels fast, and when Lily came home and told Violet the news that Nathan had left for good, Violet was devastated. Although Nathan had told her he was going, she had hoped he might have changed his mind.

Violet blinked back tears as she sat opposite her cousin at the kitchen table. "He didn't even say goodbye to me. He can't have thought I was an important person in his life not to do that. I mean... Oh, I don't know."

"It might be just the opposite, Violet. Maybe he thought so much of you that he couldn't bear to say goodbye."

"That's nice of you to say. I don't know if it's true."

"Anyway, perhaps you should forget about him. He seems to always make you sad."

"Really?"

Lily nodded. "You seem much happier with Benjamin."

"Have you been talking to Willow?"

Lily shook her head. *"Nee."*

"She said the very same thing at your *vadder's* birthday dinner."

"Oh, well, perhaps you should listen to both of us."

"Maybe."

She didn't know why Nathan had a hold on her heart and if she couldn't explain that to herself, how would she explain it to anybody else? Benjamin had said unwise things to Nathan, but it just showed that Nathan was too easily swayed away from staying in the community and didn't know what he wanted. Everybody was right about her needing to forget about him, and she decided to make a concentrated effort on doing just that.

The following Saturday came, the day that she had agreed for Benjamin to take her out somewhere. They were going on a picnic, and Lily had helped her fill a basket with goodies for the picnic. She was still flattered that out of all the other girls in the community he could have been seeing, Benjamin had chosen her. But she couldn't help comparing everything he did and said to Nathan.

If only Nathan had been prepared to overlook other people and realize that not everybody was perfect. Even people in the community weren't perfect; it seemed like Nathan had expected everybody to be completely without fault, and that just wasn't realistic.

"It's a beautiful day, isn't it?" Benjamin said as the buggy horse clip-clopped his way down the tree-lined road.

The sky was the deepest blue, so blue that it seemed to have a purple tint to it. The fluffy white clouds were pushed along the sky by a cool breeze, which reached down to the tall grasses and wildflowers along the roadside and made them sway as the buggy passed by.

"Jah, it's a lovely day and I am looking forward to this picnic."

He glanced over at her. "Me too."

"Oh, did you bring a blanket? I think I remembered everything else but."

"I've got a couple in the back that we can use."

"Oh, good."

"Now, where is this good picnic spot that you know?"

"It's back down by that creek that we were at the other day. The one where you were trying to find stones to skim across the water." Violet giggled.

He grimaced. "I didn't see any nice grassy areas there for a picnic."

"It's up further than that spot. It's quite a distance. But it'll be worth it when we get there."

He glanced over at her. "You know what?"

"What?"

"Something tells me it's going to be a very special day."

She smiled when she looked into his handsome face. "Maybe it will be."

She directed him to the spot she had told him about. When he pulled up the buggy, he secured his horse, grabbed a blanket, and then lifted the picnic basket out of the back of the buggy.

"Lead the way," he said.

She pointed over to a grassy spot. "It doesn't look as good as I remembered it. I haven't been here for years."

"Nee, I imagined something different when you told me about it."

She gave a little giggle. "Last time I was here there was more grass. Probably because we haven't had much rain yet."

He raised his eyebrows and said in a joking, light-hearted manner, "Were you here with another man? Should I be jealous?"

She laughed as they walked on. *"Nee,* nothing like that. My *mudder* used to bring my *schweschder* and me here when we were younger. This was our special place to come. Willow and I would run and run. I don't know why we'd run so much here when we never ran at home in the fields."

When they reached a grassy patch, he placed the basket down and spread the blanket out. "I feel honored that you would bring me to a special place."

She sat down on the blanket and opened the basket. "Are you hungry yet?"

"Not just yet. Let's just sit for a while and enjoy the sunshine."

"Okay. I'll pour us a glass of cider."

"Nee, let me do it." He pulled out the bottle, unscrewed it, and poured out two glasses.

He handed one to her and since he had such a large hand, she'd no choice but to touch his fingers, which he'd seemed to deliberately spread out on the glass.

"Denke," she said as she took hold of the glass.

He leaned closer to her, and his grin widened into a smile. "It's really nice that I could come to this community and meet a girl like you."

Not knowing what to say, she took a sip of cider. Seeing that he was waiting for an answer, she said, *"Denke,* but I'm nothing special."

"You are to me, Violet."

She was embarrassed and giggled, which came out as more of a squawk. With her free hand, she put her fingertips to her lips. "I'm sorry."

"For what?"

"I don't know why, but I'm always saying or doing the wrong thing. I do and say things before I think."

He continued to stare at her. "That's what I like about you. You're honest and natural."

She took another sip of her drink because he was making her nervous.

"I can see me staying around these parts."

"Jah, you said the other day you intended to stay here."

"Violet, I know we haven't spent a great deal of time together, but I'm keen to start on the next chapter of my life. I've got my working life organized and now I'd like to get my home life the same way. I want to start a family. I was wondering what you thought about marriage."

Violet gulped and swallowed, managing to swallow the large mouthful of cider she'd just taken. "I think marriage is a good thing, of course it is."

"I mean marriage—you and me."

Chapter Sixteen

Violet's eyes grew wide. She thought he'd been hinting at marriage, but now he was no longer hinting. She hadn't expected him to propose so soon. Wouldn't they have gone on various dates and outings for months before he even thought about marriage?

"What do you say, Violet? Will you marry me?" He stared at her with his eyes glowing with so much affection that it made Violet feel uncomfortable.

Violet coughed to buy time while she thought through a response. It didn't feel right. He didn't feel right. Even though he was good looking, and polite, and everything she wanted in a man, it didn't feel right in her heart. She cleared her throat. "I feel as if I don't know you well enough to say yes or no."

He frowned, seeming not to like her answer. "What do you mean?"

"We hardly know one another. Not well enough to make a decision like that that will last a lifetime."

"What's there to know? We're both in the community and it ends the search for both of us. We'll no longer have to put any more effort into finding a marriage partner. If we marry each other, we'll be done with it all and on to the business of making *grosskinner* for my parents."

Violet's cheeks grew hot. She couldn't help but frown as she tried to follow the logic of what he'd just said. Had he meant he was proposing to her because he thought she would be the one most likely to say yes to him, and she was the easiest choice for him? He seemed more eager to be married, rather than taking time to choose his wife carefully. Love seemed unimportant to him, not as important as getting his parents *grosskinner.*

"I'm in no hurry to get married and I need to get to know you a great deal better before I can say whether we're a good match."

"Well, what are you looking for in a husband, Violet?"

"I'm looking for love, of course. Isn't that what everyone looks for?"

He shook his head and snarled, "Love grows after marriage, Violet. Didn't your *mudder* ever teach you anything?"

His pleasantness was gone and his voice had more than a hint of a snarky tone to it. She was disappointed at his response. There was certainly a different side to Benjamin. If she married him, she was sure he was the type of man who would not let her have a say in anything. "My *mudder* taught me everything I need to know. Regardless of who says what, I won't marry anybody unless I'm in love with him."

He almost scoffed as he laughed. "I think you're being rather naive and childish, Violet. You come across as mature and sensible but you're really just a child. Love like you're looking for does not exist. It's the stuff of trashy romance novels."

She stared at him. "It's not. The Bible is full of stories of love." Seeing him still staring at her blankly, she didn't even bother to recount to him all the love stories she could name from the Bible. Her words would be lost on him. "Anyway, we're each entitled to our own opinion."

He sprang to his feet. "I will withdraw that offer of marriage. I've got no intention of being involved with an argumentative woman. A woman should follow where a man leads without question." He shook his head at her as he towered above her.

She shielded her eyes from the sun as she looked up at him. Violet was willing to follow, but didn't know about the part that involved not questioning the man she was following. For her to follow someone, she would need to be confident that everything lined up with the Word Of God and plain old common sense. Because of his aggressive attitude, she kept her thoughts to herself.

He continued, "I didn't think you were that kind of person, Violet. I'm quite surprised."

It was irritating her so much that she couldn't keep quiet any longer. "I'm not an argumentative person. Are you looking for a woman who doesn't have any opinions? Someone who would say yes as soon as you asked her to marry you, without knowing each other?"

"It happens. Many people make quick marriages. It's romantic. Isn't that the type of thing you want?"

"Well, that's fine for them, I guess, for the people who want quick marriage, but I'm not one of those people. Regarding romance—yes, I do want that, but we don't agree on what's romantic."

"A quick marriage is romantic. It means we're both sure."

What he was suggesting, in her mind, was stupidity and far from romantic. He had no idea the kind of person she was. "Anyway, sit down and let's eat." Violet wished she hadn't taken so much trouble preparing the food. This was going to be an awkward picnic. When he didn't sit down and instead continued to stare down at her, she said, "Well, we best not let this food go to waste." She opened the lid of the basket that he'd closed when he'd replaced the bottle of cider.

"I'm not hungry. I'm going for a walk." He strode away.

When he was out of sight, she felt bad that things had soured. Turning her attention to the food, she pulled out a piece of fried chicken. "Special day indeed!" she said aloud to herself. She took a bite, actually feeling better to eat alone.

Violet was onto her third piece of fried chicken when Benjamin walked back and sat down on the blanket.

"I'm sorry for my behavior, Violet. I let anger get the better of me."

Violet swallowed the mouthful of chicken and wiped her greasy hands on a paper napkin. "That's okay. We all get upset about things from time to time." She dabbed the napkin around her mouth, pleased that he'd been man enough to apologize for his outburst.

"You're right about getting to know each other a little better first."

She nodded and her heart sank as she realized she wasn't off the hook, and now she was convinced that they were totally unsuited. But how could she get out of this without hurting his feelings?

"Have you met any other girls you like since you've been here?"

He stared at her for a moment before he answered, "Why would you ask me something like that?"

His tone indicated that he didn't like her question. Violet shrugged her shoulders. "I just thought maybe you should get to know some other girls before… I don't know, I mean…"

"I see what you mean. Are you trying to let me know you're not interested in me?"

She bit the inside of her lip. That was exactly what she was trying to do, but it sounded awful the way he said it. "I guess I'm just not ready to get married."

"Not ready yet? Exactly how old are you, Violet?"

"I'm eighteen."

He leaned back as though in shock. "Oh! I thought you were much older than that."

She pushed her glasses further up the bridge of her nose. "How old did you think I was?"

"I don't know, twenty-three to twenty-six, maybe. I thought you would've turned down many offers of marriage by now. That explains why you're so immature."

Violet was more upset about him thinking she looked old rather than him saying he thought her immature. His words were so odd it crossed her mind that he might be joking. Studying his face, she saw no hint of a smile. Those must've been his true thoughts.

It was starting to make sense why he thought she would say yes to him so quickly, if he thought she was that old. It would mean she'd been passed over by other men and was getting desperate to marry. "Does age make a difference to you?"

"I had hoped to marry someone closer to my own age."

"And how old are you?" Violet asked.

"I'm twenty eight. There were no women back home

and when I say none, I literally mean none. Now that I'm here, I want to get married as soon as possible." He looked at her intently. "Do you see something wrong in that?"

"*Nee.* But I see that I'm not the right one for you."

"*Jah,* now I can see that you're too young for me."

"*Jah,*" Violet agreed in a quiet voice.

He opened the lid of the picnic basket, seeming far more relaxed now. "Ah, good. You've left some chicken for me," he said as he glanced down at all the chicken bones that Violet had piled up.

Violet relaxed too, and had to laugh. "Just as well you came back when you did."

The ride back to Lily's house wasn't quite as awkward as Violet had thought it might be. Benjamin had gotten over whatever had been troubling him and was talking more freely, as though they'd never exchanged a cross word or had any kind of misunderstanding.

When he stopped the buggy at Elijah and Lily's house and didn't make a move to get out, she felt obliged out of politeness to ask, "Are you coming inside?"

He shook his head. "*Nee.* I should help you with the basket, though." He made to get out of the buggy.

"Don't. I can manage it. It's a lot lighter now that you ate all the chicken," she said with a little giggle. She pulled the basket from the back of the buggy, pleased that they were back on good terms and pleased that he knew she was no longer interested in him. "Bye, Benjamin."

"I'll see you 'round, Violet."

The buggy moved away, and she walked up to the door of the house, hoping Lily was home. When Violet pushed open the door, she saw Lily sitting on the couch, doing some of her needlework. She jumped up when Violet came through the door.

"Let me take that from you." She hurried to take the basket out of her hands.

"I can do it, Lily."

"So can I. Benjamin didn't come in, I see?" Lily pulled the basket out of Violet's hands.

"He probably thought Elijah wasn't home. Anyway, the picnic took long enough. Do you think you'd be able to drive me home?"

"Are you homesick?"

"A little."

"Can't you just stay for a few more days? Daisy will be back next week and I'll be lonely until then."

Violet giggled at Lily's sad face. It must've been hard to be a twin and be without the other. "Okay I'll stay until Lily…sorry, until Daisy comes back."

Lily threw her arms around her and hugged her tightly. *"Denke,* Violet. I love having you here."

"I don't know why I called you Daisy just now."

Lily swiped a hand in the air. "Don't worry about it. Do you think that's never happened before?"

"I guess it probably has, once or twice." Violet giggled.

"More like every single day of our lives."

"Anyway, I've enjoyed being here. It's been lovely and I really needed the break. A few more days sounds like a good thing for both of us."

"That's good. I'll empty this out." Lily took the basket into the kitchen and proceeded to toss out the garbage.

"I can do that, Lily. You sit down and talk to me."

"Okay." Lily sat down at the kitchen table. "I haven't

asked, and I've been waiting for you to tell me, but since you haven't—what happened at the picnic?"

Violet looked over at her, and saw her anxiously waiting to hear. "Well, you can't tell anybody."

"Not even Daisy?"

"I'm guessing you tell Daisy absolutely everything?"

"Absolutely everything, and probably things that I shouldn't." Lily giggled.

"Okay, I suppose you can tell Daisy because I don't think she'll tell anyone else."

"You're right, she wouldn't," Lily answered quickly.

"It didn't go well." Violet left off what she was doing and sat down opposite Lily. "It was actually dreadful. He asked me to marry him, and then he could see I didn't want to."

Lily gasped. "That's fast."

"Exactly what I thought, and I said so…and I think I offended him. Anyway, we talked things through and now we're back to being friends." Violet left out the part about Benjamin thinking she was well into her twenties.

"Well, at least you've sorted that out now, that he's not the man for you."

"I'm glad you agree with me."

"I thought he was good for you, but now after what you told me, I guess he's not. Otherwise, you'd be upset and you're not, are you?"

Violet shook her head. "I'm relieved. I think I was forcing myself to go out with him. Like I was trying to talk myself into liking him in a romantic way."

"You just need to forget about men for a while."

"Well, *jah,* I just need a break from them." Violet stood up and went back to taking things out of the basket. "I'm just upset that Nathan didn't even say goodbye to me."

"What happened to forgetting about men?"

Violet sighed. *"Jah,* I know, that's what I'm doing—forgetting. I'm forgetting about Nathan and forgetting about Benjamin."

"Now are you sure you won't be sad if Benjamin marries someone else?"

"I'll be happy for him."

Lily scrunched up her face. "Won't you be even a little bit sad?"

"Nee. I'll be glad. He's not the man for me."

And that's exactly what Benjamin did; he married someone else after Violet refused him. Months later, Benjamin proposed to Bessy, a twenty-eight-year-old woman. She'd been a jilted bride engaged to Thomas Egberger, who'd broken off their engagement only weeks before the wedding, and then he quickly married Sarah King, a much younger and prettier version of Bessy.

Now Bessy had something to smile about, because she had managed to find a good man in Benjamin. Violet was happy for both of them. Maybe Bessy thought their approaching quick marriage was romantic and she'd blindly follow his lead and give Benjamin's parents many grandchildren. Violet was happy it hadn't been she who was going to marry him.

Nancy sat across from Nerida and Valerie when they were having a quick break from serving the food at the Sunday meeting when Benjamin and Bessy's approaching wedding was announced.

"That was a huge failure, Nancy. Didn't you think Benjamin and Violet were a match?"

"I had hoped so."

"There is someone different for Violet," Valerie said.

"I would hope so, but she doesn't seem interested in anybody."

Nancy patted her sister's hand. "There's still time. Maybe we should start early with Willow."

"Nee, I'd rather leave things be. I'm disappointed that things didn't go according to plan with Violet."

"Things don't always go according to plan. And when that happens, we have to adjust with things and change our plans," Nancy said.

Nerida shook her head. "I don't know. Maybe we should've just let things be rather than trying to push a man on her. Let her make her own choice."

"That's not what you said the other day."

"I don't like a certain man she was giving attention to. That was the problem."

"There's nothing wrong with Nathan," Valerie said. "He's a lovely young man. He just needs to find his way and work himself out. He's had a tough time of things with his father the way he was. His mother was too soft and gentle to be with a man like that."

"I don't want his problems to become Violet's. I'm not saying there's anything wrong with him, but…"

"He's left the community now so there's nothing to talk about," Nancy said, appearing a little annoyed with her sister.

"I have a feeling he'll come back and stay for good." Valerie smiled.

Nerida stared at Valerie. "I hope you haven't said that to my *dochder.* Maybe she's waiting for that to happen."

"*Nee,* I'd never say anything of the kind to her. I wouldn't want to get her hopes up."

As soon as Valerie said that, Nerida knew for certain that Violet liked Nathan. That gave Nerida more reason to be worried because he'd had a troubled family life. What would he know about raising children properly? He had no examples to go by and that wasn't good for Violet. If he'd been raised in a different family, Nerida might have felt differently about him.

They'd tried to bring Benjamin to her attention, but she had passed him by. They couldn't force her to marry someone. She had to make her own choice.

Nerida had seen firsthand what happened when someone made a wrong marriage, and she didn't want that to happen to her eldest daughter. All her nieces had made good marriages and she wanted the same for Violet. Surely that wasn't too much to expect. Nathan had been gone for months and it didn't look like he was coming back, so it was no use even considering him.

Across town, Nathan still hadn't forgotten his feelings for Violet, the girl he'd grown up with. As much as he could, he pushed Violet out of his mind. At lunchtime, instead of eating lunch in the workshop with the other men, he drove off by himself. He couldn't stand to listen to them talk about their girlfriends and wives. It always made him feel so alone, like he was the only one in the world with no living relatives. He figured he had some relations somewhere, but he'd never met them. He stopped at a nearby diner.

After he'd sat in a booth and placed his order, he leaned over and grabbed a couple of newspapers off the empty table nearby. To his astonishment, one of them was an Amish newspaper. He thumbed his way through it. Then a name caught his eye. It was Benjamin Hostetler. He was devastated to see Benjamin was getting married. His heart pounded and he hoped Benjamin wasn't marrying Violet. There was a section of the paper missing, but the date of the paper was on the bottom. It was a recent paper so the wedding wouldn't have yet taken place. Someone had ripped a section out of the paper and the name of Benjamin's bride was missing.

He pushed the newspaper away from him to the other side of the table and held his head in his hands. *Surely she wouldn't marry him.*

Chapter Seventeen

Things had been going well for Nathan. He had been promoted at work to foreman, which meant a huge pay increase. With the rent coming in from his mother's house, which he had decided to keep rather than sell, he was doing well all 'round.

What played on his mind was the fact that he didn't belong in the English world, and deep down he saw himself as an Amish man. He still held all the beliefs and principles that he'd been raised with, keeping them in his heart.

He'd thought long and hard about returning to the community. He'd hardened his heart somewhat when the newcomer, Benjamin, had told him off, telling him he should only return for the right reasons and not for Violet alone. After being away from the community for a while, he realized that Benjamin had annoyed him because his words had been right. Now after much consideration, he knew that he had to return because it was the right thing for him, and the right thing in God's sight.

The wedding announcement for Benjamin Hostetler was a horrid thing if it was Violet he was intending to marry. How would he be able to return to the community knowing Violet was married to someone else? It should've been him.

As he sat there at the table of the diner trying to adjust to the shock of Violet possibly marrying another, her words rang through his head. He had to come back to the community for himself and for the sake of his relationship with *Gott* and not for her. His first instinct was to get in his car and drive to see her and make sure she wasn't going to marry Benjamin, but he stopped himself. The wedding wasn't for a while.

It was ten on a Saturday morning when Nathan walked out of his bedroom in the house that he shared with two other young men. When he reached the living room, he saw his two housemates had fallen asleep—one on each couch.

There were empty beer cans and empty pizza boxes lying around, tossed carelessly over the floor. There was an Xbox game still playing and one of his housemates still had a controller in his hand. He shook his head. This was not the life he wanted. He had to make a change.

He decided then and there to go and visit his good friend Valerie. She was the one who'd helped with his mother's funeral. While he showered and got ready, he decided to call in at Nancy's house first, and if she was available, he'd drive her over to Valerie's house. He knew those two Amish ladies were full of wisdom and he felt the need to talk with someone who had his best interests at heart. He wouldn't mention Violet at all unless they brought up her name.

Two hours later, he was knocking on Nancy's door.

Hezekiah opened the door and he smiled when he saw him, offering his hand to shake.

"Nathan, it's so good to see you. Come inside."

Before Nathan could say anything, he was being pulled inside Hezekiah Yoder's house.

"It's nice to see you too, Hezekiah."

Hezekiah called out to Nancy. "Nancy, we've got Nathan Beiler here."

Nathan looked up when he saw Nancy walking down the stairs.

"Nathan, it's so good to see you! What have you been doing with yourself?"

Nathan gave a small chuckle. "I told you I would visit you one day, so here I am."

"Valerie and I were talking about you just the other day."

"I hope you were saying good things," he said with a laugh.

"Of course we were. Sit down and I'll make you a cup of tea."

He glanced at Hezekiah and then back at Nancy. "I had hoped we might go and see Valerie? I've got my car here. I could drive us."

"I've got things to do today," Hezekiah said, "but you go right ahead, Nancy."

"Okay. Let's go, then. Oh, I hope she's home. She'll be so upset to miss you if she's not."

Nathan said goodbye to Hezekiah, still pleased that the deacon had been pleased to see him.

As Nathan walked out to the car with Nancy, she repeated, "I hope she's home. She's usually home on a Saturday."

When they got into the car, and after they both

buckled their seatbelts, Nathan couldn't stop himself from asking the one thing he promised himself he wouldn't. "How's Violet?"

"She's not married, if that's what you mean."

He laughed and started up the car. Then he realized how much tension he was holding in his body as it lifted off him and floated away. "You can see right through me."

"Nothing much gets past me. I've had six *kinner,* don't forget."

"I'll have to remember that. I was somewhere the other day and came across an Amish newspaper. I saw Benjamin Hostetler was getting married but the part where it said who he was marrying was missing. I thought he might have married Violet."

Nancy chuckled. *"Nee.* She didn't like him like we thought she might."

"That's good."

He saw Nancy smiling at him out of the corner of his eye as he concentrated on driving.

"Good for who?" Nancy asked.

"Me, of course, and for her too."

Valerie was at home, and minutes later they were all sitting around the kitchen table with hot tea and cookies.

"These are the best cookies I've had since I don't know when, Valerie."

Valerie giggled. "They're just plain old sugar cookies."

Nancy leaned in toward him. "Nathan, we know you didn't come here to talk about cookies. As much as we love you visiting us, I can't help the feeling that you have something on your mind. Apart from what we talked about in the car."

A smile twitched at his lips. "I've been thinking about coming back to the community for good. I want to make my life matter for something. I know that's what *Gott* would have me do."

The ladies looked delighted.

"That's *wunderbaar!*" Valerie said, her face beaming.

"It certainly is. We've been praying for you, Nathan."

"*Denke.* I've needed it; I can tell you that."

"Wait a minute. Are you coming back, or are you only thinking about it?" Valerie asked.

"I'm on the verge of coming back and I just wanted to talk to the both of you to sort out the last of my doubts."

"Go ahead. We'll help you wherever we can."

"I just have a few nagging things at the back of my mind. I don't know if I'm being petty-minded or not."

"Go on," Nancy said, leaning forward.

"It started back when my father was having a hard time with his drinking. You probably know it got worse and worse, and I thought the community could do a bit more in the way of support rather than shunning him. It seemed to me that he was shunned, and then gossiped about. I was a teenager at the time of his last shunning, but I was still fully aware of what was going on."

"And you left not long after your father died," Valerie stated.

"I did." Nathan nodded. "I just didn't want to be around people like that who I thought had done the wrong thing by him, but then when my mother died I saw a different side of most of the people in the community. Almost everyone was supportive, including the bishop and his wife. It makes me wonder if I only saw the bad side of people when my father was going through his trials."

"We often can only see the bad side of things instead of seeing the good side. The shunning is done so people see their errors. It's just the way things are done."

"I know what it's for, but it seems so against the teachings of love, forgiveness, and understanding."

"It's so people can see their errors."

"I don't think it achieves that," Nathan said.

"Nothing's perfect, Nathan, and as long as the church, the Body of Christ on earth, is full of people, it will not be perfect. I'm not saying that shunning's right or wrong; it might be right for some and not others. I don't know," Nancy said.

"The thing is," Nathan said. "I've come to realize that no one's perfect, and everybody has their good points and bad points. And then there are some people who seem to like to talk about people, but that's just how these people are and they're only in the minority. I shouldn't have held such a grudge."

"It sounds like you're sorting your way through things," Valerie said.

Nancy said, "So are you coming back to the community?"

He smiled and nodded. "Yes. I'll drive over to the bishop's house today and speak with him. I'll have to find someone to take my place in the house I'm leasing, and I don't know what to do about my job. I'll talk to the bishop about that. I might be able to stay in my job. I just got a promotion at the building company where I work and now I'm the foreman."

"I don't see any reason why you wouldn't be able to keep that job," Valerie said.

"You can live with us. Hezekiah will be happy to have another man around. We've got a big *haus* and plenty of spare bedrooms."

"Denke, Nancy. That's very generous of you, but the people who are leasing my mother's house are moving out soon, so that's perfect timing."

"Things always have a way of working themselves out, but you'll have to start calling it your house, Nathan."

He slowly nodded. "It's hard to get my head around that."

"Violet will be so happy that you're coming back," Valerie said.

He raised his eyebrows. "I'd rather have her not know for the moment."

"You're not going to change your mind, are you?" Valerie asked. "Is that why you don't want us to say anything?"

He laughed. *"Nee.* I don't want… I don't know why, but I don't want to tell her just yet. I think I'd rather tell her in person."

"We won't say anything if you don't want us to."

"Denke. Well, I'd better make a move if I'm going to see the bishop." He stood up. "Do you want to stay on here, Nancy, or do you want me to drive you home?"

"I might stay on here with Valerie."

"Jah, I'll drive her home later *denke,* Nathan."

"Thank you both for the talk. It was good to get some things off my chest and just talking about things has made me clearer on what I need to do. I have no one to talk to about anything, really. Except friends my age, and they're really no help at all. I can't talk to them about any of this stuff."

"We all need someone we can talk with," Valerie said with a smile.

"Talk to either of us at any time," Nancy said.

"Denke." He stood up and they walked him to the door.

When he got into his car and drove away, he realized he'd have to sell his car and go back to using a horse and buggy. At least his mother's house had a barn. It was packed full of the furniture out of the house, but as soon as the tenants left, he'd get organized.

Chapter Eighteen

Days later, Violet sat in Bessy's parents' home and watched Benjamin and Bessy get married. She realized that it could've been her standing up there with Benjamin and she was glad it wasn't. Even though Nathan had left the community months ago, he was still very much on her mind.

When the ceremony was over, everybody left the house so the men could take out the long benches and replace them with tables for the wedding breakfast. No sooner than she had walked outside with Willow, she looked up and locked eyes with Nathan Beiler.

She opened her mouth in shock while she heard Willow say hello to him. He said hello back to Willow, his eyes scarcely leaving Violet's. He looked the same except he was a little heavier and he was wearing Amish clothes—the black pants and white shirt with black suspenders that all the men at the wedding were wearing.

"Nathan! What are you doing here?" she said when she found her voice.

"I'm back."

"What do you mean you're back?"

"I'm back in the community for good."

She could feel her heart pound, and felt as though she would faint. In that moment, she wasn't aware of anybody around her and she and Nathan might as well have been the only two people in the world. When people brushed past her, she became aware of her surroundings.

He nodded to the edge of the yard. "Let's go over here."

She followed him across the lawn, and he stopped and turned around to face her.

"I've done a lot of thinking about everything. I'm back officially. I've spoken to the bishop and everything. I'm taking the instructions and getting baptized."

It was the best news she'd ever heard.

"And it has nothing to do with you," he added with a smile, referring to what Benjamin had said to him many months ago.

She gave a little giggle. "That's good to know. Where will you be staying?"

"I'm moving back into my *mudder's haus.*"

"I thought you sold it."

"I was going to, but I changed my mind and leased it instead."

"Well, that's good news."

"I don't mind telling you that when I heard Benjamin was getting married I had to hold my breath. I thought it might be you he was marrying."

She didn't tell him that it very well could've been. "I'm not close to being married. What about you?"

"Me?" He shook his head. "I've just been working hard. I got a promotion to foreman. The bishop said I can stay working there. I thought I might have to leave, but there are others working for *Englischers.*"

"You've spoken to the bishop?" As soon as she asked the question, she remembered he'd already said that.

"Of course I have. I'm officially back in the community and I'll be baptized as soon as I can."

It was real! He was making a commitment to God and a commitment to the community by being baptized.

He looked out over the crowd. "I should go and say hello to a few people."

"Jah, good idea."

He left her standing there and walked into the crowd. It surprised her that he had someone to say hello to and while she was wondering who that might be, Willow ran up to her.

"What did he say, Violet?"

She kept staring after him, now on her tiptoes to keep her eyes on him. "He's back; he's getting baptized."

"For good?" Willow asked.

"Jah."

Willow continued to chatter away about Nathan, but Violet wasn't listening. She was a little concerned that Nathan hadn't said anything personal to her. It seemed like he still liked her from the little he'd said. He might have wanted to wait awhile before pursuing a relationship with her. The only thing she could do was wait, pray, and be patient.

Violet's stomach churned so much she hoped that she wouldn't be sick. She turned to Willow. "I don't think I can stay here."

Willow frowned, making lines in her young forehead. "You have to."

Violet put her hand over her stomach. "I feel sick now."

"Sick because of Nathan?"

"I suppose so; it was a shock to see him here."

"If love makes you sick, I don't want any part of it."

"Don't be silly, Willow. I just want to go home."

"Then *Mamm* and *Dat* will want to know why, and do you want to tell them it's because you saw Nathan?"

Violet shook her head. *"Nee,* I couldn't tell them that."

"You're just gonna have to suffer through it."

And that's just what Violet did. She sat down at a table, staying in the same seat throughout the wedding breakfast, and didn't make an effort to speak with anyone. When the crowd thinned and people were leaving, she didn't see Nathan anywhere. He'd gone home without saying goodbye.

Chapter Nineteen

"Why didn't anyone tell me that Nathan was coming back to the community?" Violet asked her mother when she walked into the kitchen the next morning.

Her mother spun around from the stove. "I heard something, but it's not my place to carry on gossip."

"Who told you?"

"I suppose it won't hurt to tell you now."

"Go on."

"He came by and talked to Nancy and Valerie a few days back. He said he was coming back but he wanted to keep it quiet."

Violet pulled a face. "I wish someone would have said."

"What difference would that have made?"

"I would've been warned. It was a shock to see him there yesterday at the wedding. I felt a little foolish that I didn't know he was coming back."

"I don't see why that would make you feel foolish."

Violet slumped into the chair at the kitchen table.

"Cheer up. I'll make you some pancakes."

Violet nodded.

"You still like him?" her mother asked.

"Jah, I do, but I don't know if anything will come of it."

"Why's that?"

Violet sighed. She didn't want to say too much to her mother. She couldn't work out whether her mother approved of him or not. She seemed to be wavering and didn't seem like the same woman who said he had the devil in him. When it came to matters of the heart, Violet preferred to talk to Aunt Nancy, or to Valerie. "Do you know what Aunt Nancy is doing today?"

"I don't know. Shall we visit her this morning when Willow wakes?"

Violet pouted. "Do you mind if I go by myself?"

Her mother lifted her head up from mixing pancake batter, with the wooden spoon frozen above the bowl. "If that's what you want to do."

"You don't mind?"

"I don't mind at all."

"Where are you going?" Willow asked as she walked into the room yawning.

"I'm going over to see Aunt Nancy by myself this morning."

Willow placed her hands on her hips. "That's not fair. Why can't I come too?"

Their mother interrupted, "Because you and I have a lot of work to do, Willow."

"Doesn't Violet have work she needs to do as well?"

"Violet has a job; that's why she doesn't have to do as many chores at home as we do."

Willow crossed her arms over her chest and huffed. "It's only a part-time job."

"Sit down and I'll make you some pancakes," their mother said.

"Maybe I'll get a job too," Willow said, sitting down heavily.

When Violet arrived at Nancy's house, she knocked on the door and it was flung open quickly.

Nancy stood there and when she saw her, looked beyond her. "Violet, it's lovely to see you. Is your *mudder* here?"

"Nee, I came alone because I wanted to talk to you in private. Are you alone?"

Nancy stepped back to let her through.

"Let's sit in the living room."

Once they were seated, Violet began, "I feel a little silly coming here."

"You should never feel like that. What's the problem?"

"It's about Nathan. You knew he was coming back?"

"Jah, he visited me a few days back. Then I rode in his car with him over to talk to Valerie."

"He told you he was coming back?"

"He did, but at the same time, he said he didn't want anyone to know. After he talked to us he went right to the bishop."

Violet smiled. "I'm glad he's back."

"Did you only find out at the wedding?"

"Jah, that's why I was so surprised and I wondered why you wouldn't have told me. *Mamm* said this morning that both you and Valerie knew about it. That explains things."

Nancy laughed. "Did you come here to be mad at me?"

"Not at all! I just wanted to know how everything evolved."

"And he's moved into his mother's *haus.*"

Violet nodded. *"Jah,* he told me that."

"Why don't we visit him now?"

"Nee, I couldn't do that." Violet shook her head. That would be the last thing she wanted to do.

"Why not?"

"I'd be too nervous to do that."

"C'mon. Let's go and see him."

Violet shook her head again. *"Nee.* Wouldn't he be working?"

"Jah, I forgot about that. He would be. You're not working today?"

"Nee." Violet stood up. "I'm sorry. Maybe I shouldn't have come."

Nancy stood up. "I'm glad you did."

"I should be getting back in case *Mamm* needs the buggy or something."

"Okay. Visit me anytime. You don't have to wait for your *mudder.*"

Violet swung around to face her aunt. "Oh, and please don't say anything to Nathan. I wouldn't want him to know that I'm asking about him."

Nancy laughed. "Your secret's safe with me."

Violet hugged her aunt goodbye and left the house. As soon as she was down to the end of the driveway, she turned her buggy onto the open road and had her horse break into a trot. There was something soothing about being by herself in a buggy, feeling the cool breeze across her face.

She was happily looking over to the side of the road at all the branches losing their leaves and the soft leaves falling about the buggy. When she turned her attention back to the road, she saw another buggy up ahead. Squinting hard, she saw that it was Nathan in the buggy.

He slowed his buggy as he approached her, and she slowed her horse to a walk. When they drew level, they both stopped.

"What are you doing out this way?" she asked.

"I was looking for you. I called at your place, and they said you were at Nancy's *haus.*"

"Oh, aren't you working today?"

"I was. I'm having some time off. I organized my workers to do without me for a few hours." He chuckled.

"What did you want to see me about?"

"Are you in a hurry?"

"Nee. I'm just heading back home."

"Can we talk?"

"Jah. Do you want to follow me back home?"

"I'll turn my horse around and we can pull up over there." He pointed behind him where there was a clearing to the side of the road.

She walked her horse off the road. All the while her heart pumped hard as she wondered what he had to say. What worried her most was the serious look on his face. Perhaps he was still upset with what Benjamin had said to him back at her uncle's birthday dinner. Maybe she should've told Benjamin to stop what he was saying and keep out of things.

When they had both stepped out of their buggies, he walked over to her.

"I couldn't concentrate at work today. I had to come and see you."

She stared at him in silence, wondering what was so important, and waited for him to continue.

"I came to find you because I wanted to let you know that I came back for the right reasons."

"I'm sorry, Nathan. I should've told Benjamin to mind his own business back then."

He laughed. "I'm not concerned about him—not for a moment. No matter what might or might not happen between us later, I came back for me and only me."

She heaved a relieved sigh. *"Denke,* it means a lot to hear you say that. I'm glad you told me."

He looked down at the ground for a moment and when he looked up at her, he said, "It's good to see you again, Violet."

"It's good to see you, too."

"I've been out for too long. I guess I never should've left. Anger and resentment can take a hold of someone. For the next few months, I'm going to concentrate on getting grounded back into the community."

She nodded.

He chuckled. "That's the bishop's suggestion. I guess he knows what he's talking about. Anyway, how have you been?"

She nodded. "I've been good."

"Anything new happening in your life?"

"Nee. Just the same kinds of things have been happening as before." She gave a little giggle, embarrassed at what she'd just said. It sounded stupid. "I still work part-time, but I've got an extra day a week, now."

"Good. How are your *familye?* I didn't get a chance to say hello to them on Sunday."

"They're good. Just the same as always. Nothing's changed since you left."

"It's kind of comforting to know that everything

stays the same. I feel more peaceful since I've made the decision to move back."

"How do you like moving back into the *haus?"*

"I've made a start on bringing some of it up to date. And I've painted the bedrooms a lighter color. That makes a big difference. You should come and see it sometime."

"Okay. I'd love to see it." She was a little upset that she hadn't had an input on the color of the paint. If she was closer with him, he might have asked. "Let me know when it's all finished."

He nodded. "I will."

They stood looking at each other for a moment before Violet felt the awkwardness in the silence. "I should go."

"Okay."

He followed her to her buggy. When she climbed up, he looked up at her. "I'll see you soon, I guess."

"Jah. You will." She pointed her horse homeward and clicked him forward.

He suddenly stepped forward and grabbed the horse's harness. "Wait, Violet."

She stared down at him, shocked at his sudden action. Nathan's face looked pained and she wondered whether her horse had stomped on his foot. "What's wrong?"

Chapter Twenty

"I need to say something else." He held out his hand and she looked at it.

Then she felt silly when she realized he wanted her to put her hand in his. When she did so, he held her hand tight.

"Come down and talk to me."

She stepped down from the buggy while he kept hold of her hand.

"What is it, Nathan?"

She noticed that he swallowed hard, and then he looked up to the sky, and then he looked into her eyes.

"Violet, I've been in love with you all my life. It was extremely hard for me to work out whether I wanted to come back to the community for you, or for myself. I've now realized that I can't separate the two and that can only mean that…we're meant to be together." He smiled. "I hope you feel something toward me or I'll feel extremely…extremely…like an idiot."

She could scarcely believe what she heard and stared at him while she gathered her thoughts.

He shook his head. "I wanted to wait until I'd been

back for a few months to say this to you, but I can't wait any longer. You've been on my mind every minute of every day since we met again recently when my *mudder* left me to be with *Gott.*"

She looked down at their hands clasped together. "You've been on my mind too."

His face relaxed into a smile. "It's such a relief to hear you say that, or I would've just succeeded in making a huge fool of myself."

Violet giggled.

He took hold of her hand. "Violet, you might think it's too soon, but I won't forgive myself if I delay this any longer. Will you marry me?"

"You mean it?"

He laughed. "Of course I mean it. I've never meant anything more."

"I will. I will marry you, and it's not too soon for you to have asked."

"It's not too soon for me." He shook his head. "I've loved you since we went to *schul* together. Every time I came to my *mudder's haus* to bring her food in the middle of the day, I'd look out the window hoping to catch a glimpse of you, but you never walked by."

"I had no idea."

"I pushed you out of my heart when I left the community."

"I didn't know," Violet said.

"It's true. So, you'll really marry me?"

"Jah. I really will."

He smiled and then gave her hand a little squeeze. *"Denke.* That makes me so happy, and I'll make sure that you're happy every day forever. I'll be the best husband and *vadder.*"

"I know you will. You don't have to worry so much. Just relax about things and smile more."

He chuckled. "I guess I do worry about things—everything, really. The thing I'm worried about now is your parents. I'm pretty sure they don't like me."

"They'll come 'round. They were just worried that you weren't in the community properly, and once you're baptized they'll see you're here to stay."

"Do you think so?"

She nodded.

"When shall we tell them?"

"Wait awhile, I think. At least until after you're baptized, and after they're used to seeing your face around."

"If you think that's best."

"I do." Violet didn't want to upset Nathan or her parents. If she told them she wanted to marry Nathan right now, they would probably still be against it.

"I'll do what you think is best. Can we meet on the days that you work? We could meet in town."

"Okay. I'd like that. You don't mind waiting, do you? I think it's best."

"I've waited for you for a long time, so I can wait a little longer." His face beamed with happiness.

After weeks of keeping their relationship quiet, Violet decided it was time for them to tell her parents. Her mother knew she liked Nathan and she had noticeably softened toward him, so it would be her father who would be the likely one to have a problem with the two of them wanting to marry.

It was a Tuesday night that they decided to break the news. Violet had told Nathan to come to the house at eight in the evening.

When he knocked on the door, her mother opened it.

"Hello, Nathan. Come in."

"Denke, Nerida."

Violet walked out from the kitchen and stood by Nathan's side as her father rose to his feet to shake Nathan's hand. Nathan looked over at Violet and while his lips were smiling, his eyes were filled with apprehension.

"Mamm, Dat, Nathan and I have something to tell you." Violet had told Willow what was happening that night, so Willow was listening in while hiding in the kitchen.

"We better sit down for this," her father said.

"What is it?" Nerida looked from her daughter to Nathan and back again.

After Nathan glanced at Violet, he said to John and Nerida, "I've asked Violet to marry me and she has said that she will."

Violet's father coughed in shock, and his face turned beet red. "You want to marry my *dochder?"*

"I do."

"And Violet, you want to marry Nathan?"

"Jah, Dat, I do."

"Then… I'm very happy for both of you."

Violet was amazed that her father had agreed so readily, with not one objection. She looked at her mother to see that she was stunned. "You are okay with it?" she asked her father.

"Jah. You're back fully within the community for good, Nathan?"

Nathan nodded. "I've spoken to the bishop of my intentions, and as you know, I've already been baptized.

He said he will allow us to marry in five months' time, in the next wedding season."

Violet felt dizzy and put her hand to her head.

Tears ran down Nerida's face. She got up and gave Nathan a quick kiss on each cheek and did the same for Violet.

"I'm so pleased you're both okay with this," Violet said to her parents.

"Nathan has shown that he can go through adversity. *Gott* has tested him and he's come through," her father said.

Violet smiled and nodded while Nerida excitedly suggested that they should all have hot tea.

After Nathan had stayed for a while, drinking tea and talking to her parents, Violet felt much better about everything. She didn't know what she would've done if her parents hadn't approved.

"I should get home. I've got an early morning," Nathan said, standing up.

After he had said goodnight to everyone, Violet walked him out of the house. He took hold of her hand and pulled her into the darkness, close to his buggy. He put his arms around her shoulders and pulled her close while she put her arms around his waist. It was a stolen moment.

"I've been wanting to hold you in my arms for so long," Nathan said.

Violet melted into his hard chest. "Oh, Nathan. You will stay, won't you? You'll stay in the community?"

"*Jah,* I will, Violet. I should not have let people, and my harsh judgment of them, get in the way of my worship of *Gott.* I've learned my lesson just like your *vadder* said."

Violet looked up into his eyes and he looked down into hers. He lowered his head and she closed her eyes and felt his soft lips meet hers. It was their first kiss and it was so special that Violet would remember it for the rest of her days.

The next morning, Nancy was busy with piling the washing in the gas-powered washing machine at the back of the house when she heard a buggy. She stepped around the corner to see Nerida's buggy, and she walked out to meet her.

Nerida waved excitedly and jumped down from the buggy.

"Watch your leg," Nancy reminded her.

"I'm not worried about my leg. I've got some great news. Come inside and I'll tell you."

Nerida made Nancy sit down at the kitchen table before she told her the news.

"My Violet is getting married."

Nancy put her hand to her chest. "Please let it be to Nathan."

"Jah," Nerida nearly screamed.

Relief was all Nancy felt. She had wanted the two of them to find each other. It had become clear that they'd belonged together.

"Well, aren't you going to say anything?" Nerida stared at her sister.

"I'm so happy. I feel almost like he's one of my *kinner* somehow. He's such a lovely man. I'm so glad he came back and the two of them found each other."

"And you thought Benjamin was a good match."

"Did I?" Nancy asked.

"Jah, you did."

"Hmm. I suppose that's true. I did. Everyone's entitled to one mistake."

Nerida giggled. "I didn't think you'd admit to that."

Nancy pulled a face. "I'm willing to admit I was wrong about Violet and Benjamin, and I'm glad I was."

"Me too," Nerida said with a nod.

"Violet and Nathan are a good match. I'm just upset that Lorraine wasn't here to see that her boy will be fine."

"And he's going to marry Violet."

Nancy nodded. "She'd be satisfied and happy about that. Maybe she knows what's going on with us even though she's not here."

"Maybe."

Nancy stood up. "Now, how about a cup of hot tea?"

"Always," Nerida said. "And then we've got a wedding to plan."

Nancy smiled at the thought of helping to plan her niece's wedding. She leaned over and hugged her sister, so grateful that they'd mended the rift that had kept them apart for so many years. And what's more, she couldn't even remember what the argument that had kept them apart for so long had been about.

* * * * *

SPECIAL EXCERPT FROM

Finally following his dreams of opening a bakery, Caleb Hartz hires Annie Wagler as his assistant. But they both get more than they bargain for when his runaway teenage cousin and her infant son arrive. Can they work together to care for mother and child—without falling in love?

Read on for a sneak preview of The Amish Bachelor's Baby *by Jo Ann Brown available March 2019 from Love Inspired!*

Chapter One

Harmony Creek Hollow, New York

"Don't you dare eat those socks!"

Annie Wagler leaped off the back porch as the sock carousel soared on a gust and headed toward the pen where her twin sister's goats were watching her bring in the laundry. The plastic circle, which was over twelve inches in diameter, had been clipped to the clothesline. As she'd reached for it, the wind swept it away.

Snow crunched beneath her boots, and she ducked under the clothes that hung, frozen hard, on the line. She despised bringing in laundry during the winter and having to hang the clothing over an air dryer rack inside until it thawed. She hated everything to do with laundry. Washing it, hanging it, bringing it in and folding it, ironing it and mending it. Every part of the process was more difficult in the cold.

Pulling her black wool shawl closer, she ran toward the fenced-in area where Leanna's goats roamed. She wasn't sure why they'd want to be outside on such a frigid day, but they were clumped together near where

Leanna would feed them later. Annie sometimes wondered if the goats were one part hair, hooves and eyes, and three parts stomach. They never seemed to be full.

And they would consider the cotton and wool socks a treat.

Annie yanked open the gate, making sure it was latched behind her before she ran to collect the sock carousel. She had to push curious goats aside in order to reach it. One goat was already bending to sample the airborne windfall.

"Socks are for feet, not for filling your bottomless stomachs," Annie scolded as she scooped up the socks that would have to be washed again.

The goats, in various patterns of white, black and brown, gave her both disgusted and hopeful glances. She wasn't sure why her identical twin, Leanna, liked the creatures, especially the stinky male.

Leanna had established a business selling milk and had begun experimenting with recipes for soap. Her twin hoped to sell bars at the Salem farmers market, about three miles southwest of their farm, when it reopened in the spring. As shy as her twin was, Annie wasn't sure how Leanna would handle interacting with customers.

They were mirror twins. Annie was right-handed, and Leanna left-handed. The cowlick that kept Annie's black hair from lying on her right temple was identical to Leanna's on the other side. They had matching birthmarks on their elbows, but on opposite arms. Their personalities were distinct, too. While Leanna seldom spoke up, Annie found it impossible to keep her opinions to herself.

How many times had she wished she was circumspect like her twin? For certain, too many times to count. Instead, she'd inherited her *grossmammi*'s plain-spoken ways.

Annie edged toward the gate, leaning forward so the socks were on the other side of the fence. She needed to finish bringing in the laundry so she could help her *grossmammi* and Leanna with supper. Her younger siblings were always hungry after school and work. She'd hoped their older brother, who lived past the barn, would bring his wife and *kinder* tonight, but his six-year-old son, Junior, was sick.

Keeping the sock carousel out of the goats' reach, she stretched to open the gate. One of the kids, a brown-and-white one her twin called Puddle, butted her, trying to get her attention.

Annie looked at the little goat. "If you weren't so cute, you'd be annoying, ain't so?"

"Do they talk to you when you talk to them?" asked a voice far deeper than her own.

In amazement, she looked up…and up…and up. Caleb Hartz was almost a foot taller than she was. Beneath his black, broad-brimmed hat, his blond hair fell into eyes the color of early summer grass. He had a ready smile and an easy, contagious enthusiasm.

And he was the man Leanna had her eye on.

Her sister hadn't said anything about being attracted to him, but Annie couldn't help noticing how tongue-tied Leanna was when he was nearby. He hadn't seemed to notice, and maybe Annie would have missed her sister's reactions if Annie didn't find herself a bit giddy when Caleb spoke to her. Before Caleb's sister Miriam had mentioned that Leanna seemed intrigued by her brother, Annie had been thinking…

No, it didn't matter. If Leanna had set her heart on him, Annie should remind him how *wunderbaar* her sister was. She'd do anything to have her sister happy again.

"Gute nammidaag," Annie said as she came out of the pen, being careful no goat slipped past her.

"Is it still afternoon?" He glanced toward the western horizon where the sun touched the mountaintops.

"Barely." She laughed. "I've been catching up with chores before working on supper. Would you like to eat with us this evening?"

"*Danki*, but no." Caleb clasped his hands behind him.

Annie was puzzled. Why was he uncomfortable? Usually he chatted with everyone. While he traveled from church district to church district in several states, he'd met with each of the families now living in Harmony Creek Hollow and convinced them to join him in the new community in northern New York.

"What can we do for you?" she asked when he didn't add anything else.

"I wanted to talk to you about a project I'm getting started on."

Curiosity distracted her from how the icy wind sliced through her shawl, coat and bonnet. "What project?"

"I'm opening a bakery."

"You are?" She couldn't keep the surprise out of her voice.

A *bakery*? Amish men, as a rule, didn't spend much time in the kitchen, other than to eat. Their focus was on learning farm skills or being apprenticed to a trade.

"Ja," he said, then grimaced at another blast of frigid air. His coat was closed to the collar where a scarf was edged with frost from his breath. "I stopped by to see

if you'd be interested in working for me. The bakery will be out on the main road south of the turn-off for Harmony Creek Hollow."

She set the sock carousel on a barrel. "You want to hire me? To work in your bakery?"

"I've had some success selling bread and baked goods at the farmers market in Salem. Having a shop will allow me to sell year-round, but I can't be there every day and do my work at the farm." He shivered again, and she guessed he was eager for a quick answer so he could return to his buggy. "Miriam told me you'd do a *gut* job for me."

His sister, Miriam, was one of Annie's best friends, a member of what they jokingly the Harmony Creek Spinsters' Club. Miriam hadn't mentioned anything about Caleb starting a business.

"It sounds intriguing," Annie said. "What would you expect me to do?"

"Tend the shop and handle customers. There would be some light cleaning."

"Will you expect me to do any baking? I'd want several days' warning if you're going to want me to do that."

He frowned, surprising her. It'd been a reasonable request, as she'd have to rearrange her household obligations around any extra baking. Asking Leanna would be silly. Her sister could burn air, and things that were supposed to be soft came out crunchy and vice versa. Nobody could quilt as beautifully as her twin, but the simplest tasks in the kitchen seemed to stump her.

"You've got a lot of questions," he said.

Don't ask too many questions. Don't make suggestions. She doubted Caleb would treat her as her former boyfriend had, deriding her ideas until he found one he liked so much he claimed it for his own.

His frown faded. "I may need you to help with baking sometimes."

"Will you expect me to do a daily accounting of sales?"

"*Ja.* Aren't you curious how much I'm paying you?"

She rubbed her chin with a gloved finger. "I assume it'll be a fair wage." She smiled. "You're not the sort of a man who'd take advantage of a neighbor."

His wind-buffed cheeks seemed to grow redder, and she realized her compliment had embarrassed him.

Apologizing would cause him more discomfort, so she said, "*Ja*, I'd be interested in the job."

"Then it's yours." His shoulders relaxed. "If you've got time now, I'll give you a tour of the bakery, and we can talk more about what I'd need you to do."

"Gut." The wind buffeted her, almost knocking her from her feet as she reached to keep the sock carousel from sailing away again.

"Steady there." Caleb's broad hands curved along her shoulders, keeping her on her feet.

Sensation flowed out from his palms and riveted her, as sweet as maple syrup and, at the same time, as alarming as a fire siren.

"Danki," she managed to whisper, but she wasn't sure he heard her as the wind rose again. It made her breathing sound strange.

"Are you okay?" he asked.

When she nodded, he lifted his hands away and the warmth vanished. The day seemed colder than before.

Somehow, she mumbled that she needed to let her

twin know where she was going. He wrapped his arms around himself as another blast of wind struck them.

"Hurry…anna…" The wind swallowed the rest of his words as she rushed toward the house.

She halted in midstep.

Anna?

Had Caleb thought he was talking to her twin? She'd clear everything up on their way to the bakery. She wanted the job. It was an answer to so many prayers, for God to let her find a way to help her sister be happy again, happy as Leanna had been before the man she loved married someone else without telling her.

Leanna was attracted to Caleb, and he'd be a fine match for her. Outgoing where her twin was quiet. A well-respected, handsome man whose *gut* looks would be the perfect foil for her twin's. But Leanna would be too shy to let Caleb know she was interested in him. That was where Annie could help.

God, danki *for giving me this chance to bring joy back to Leanna's life. I won't waste this opportunity You've brought to me.*

As she was sending up her grateful prayer and rushing to the house, she reminded herself of one vital thing. She must be careful not to let her own attraction to Caleb grow while they worked together.

That might be the hardest part of the job.

One task down, a hundred to go…before he started tomorrow's list.

Caleb glanced at the lead-gray sky as he moved closer to the heat box on the buggy's floor, shifting his feet under the wool blanket there. The clouds overhead were low. Snow threatened, and the dampness in the air added another layer of cold. He hoped the Wagler twin wouldn't remain in the house much longer. If he wanted to get home before the storm began, the trip to the bakery would have to be a quick one.

He hadn't been sure when he went over to the Wagler farm if he'd get a *ja* or a no to his job offer. He had to have someone to help at the bakery.

But is she Annie or Leanna?

He hadn't been sure which twin he wasn't talking to. His usual way of telling them apart was that Annie talked more than Leanna, but without both being present, he hadn't known. Not that it mattered. He had to have someone help at the bakery because he had his farm work, as well.

After almost two years of traveling and recruiting families for the Harmony Creek settlement, he finally could make his dream of opening a bakery come true. He'd turned over the community's leadership when the *Leit* ordained a minister and a deacon. It'd been the first service of the new year, and the right time to begin building the permanent leadership of their district.

He smiled in spite of the frigid wind as he glanced toward the two-story white farm house. Miriam had suggested he ask a Wagler twin to work for him. It had been a *gut* idea. The Wagler twins made heads—plain and *Englisch*—turn wherever they went. Not only were they identical, with their sleek black hair, but they were lovely. The gentle curves of their cheekbones contrasted with their pert noses. Most important, they seemed to accept everyone as they were, not wanting to change them or belittle their dreams as Verba Tice had his.

His hands tightened on the reins, and his horse looked back as if to ask what was wrong. Caleb grimaced. It was stupid to think about the woman who'd ridiculed him. Verba was in Lancaster County, and he was far away. And…

He pushed the thoughts from his head as the back door opened and a bundled-up woman emerged. Her shawl flapped behind her as she hurried—with care, because there were slippery spots everywhere—to the buggy. He slid the door on the passenger side open, and she climbed in, closing it behind her. The momentary slap of wind had been as sharp as a paring knife.

"Sorry to be so long," she said from behind a thick blue scarf. "My *grossmammi* asked me to get some canned fruit from the cellar."

"It's fine." Which twin was sitting beside him? Too late, he realized he should have asked straightaway by the goats' pen.

How could he ask now?

Giving his brown horse, Dusty, a gentle slap of the reins, he turned the buggy and headed toward the road. He tried to think of something that would lead to a clue about which Wagler twin was half hidden behind the scarf. He didn't want to talk about the weather. It was a grim subject in the midst of a March cold snap. What if he talked about the April auction to support the local volunteer fire department? The *Englisch* firefighters found it amusing when the plain volunteers called it a "mud sale." He wondered if the ground would thaw enough to let the event live up to its name.

"Caleb?"

He wanted to cheer when she broke the silence. *"Ja?"*

"You know I'm *Annie* Wagler, ain't so?"

"Ja." He did now.

"I wanted to make sure, because people mix us up,

and I didn't want you to think you had to give me the job if you'd intended to hire Leanna."

She *was* plainspoken. He prayed that would be *gut* in his shop, because he wasn't going to renege on his offer. It could be embarrassing for her, and him, and the thought of the humiliation he'd endured at Verba's hands stung.

And one thing hadn't changed: he needed help at the bakery. It shouldn't matter which twin worked for him.

Who are you trying to fool? nagged a tiny voice inside his head. The one that spoke up when he was trying to ignore his own thoughts.

Like thoughts of how right it had felt to put his hands on Annie's shoulders as he kept her from falling in the barnyard. He didn't want to recall how his heart had beat faster when her blue-green eyes had gazed up at him.

He must keep a barrier between him and any attractive woman. Getting beguiled as he had with Verba, who'd claimed to love him before she tried to change everything about him, would be stupid.

"Do you and your sister try to confuse people on purpose?" Caleb asked to force his thoughts aside.

"We did when we were *kinder*. Once we realized people couldn't tell us apart, we took advantage of it at school. I was better at arithmetic and Leanna excelled in spelling, so sometimes I'd go to the teacher to do Leanna's math problems as well as my own. She'd do the same with spelling."

"You cheated?"

"Not on written tests or desk work. Just when the teacher wasn't paying attention."

He laughed. "The other scholars never tattled on you?"

"They wouldn't get any of *Grossmammi*'s delicious cookies if they did."

"I didn't realize we had a pair of criminal masterminds in our midst."

"Very retired criminal masterminds." She smiled. "Our nice, neat plan didn't last long. A new teacher came when we were in fourth grade, and she kept much better track of us. Our days of posing as each other came to a quick end."

"So you had to learn to spell on your own?"

"And Leanna did her arithmetic problems. She realized she had a real aptitude for it and surpassed me the following year." Annie hesitated, then said, "I'm sure the whole thing was my idea. Leanna always went along with me."

He glanced at her. She was regarding him as if willing him to accept her words. He wondered why it mattered to her. For a moment, he sensed she was struggling with something big.

Again he shut down his thoughts. Annie was his employee, and it'd be better to keep some distance between them.

"So you're now the better speller?" Caleb asked, glad his tone was light.

She laughed. "I don't know. We haven't had a spelling bee in a long time."

"Maybe we should have one. I read somewhere that *Englisch* pioneers used to hold spelling bees for entertainment." He gave her a grin. "Something we could do in our spare time."

"When we get some."

Miriam had told him how much fun she had with the Wagler twins, but he hadn't known Annie possessed a dry sense of humor. She wasn't trying to flirt with him, either, and he'd heard several of the community's bachelors saying Leanna was eager to marry. Maybe asking Annie instead of her twin hadn't been such a mistake, after all.

When they reached the main road, Caleb held Dusty back. Traffic sped past. Most cars were headed to ski resorts in Vermont, and the drivers couldn't wait to reach the slopes. Local drivers complained tourists drove along the uneven, twisting country roads as if they were interstates.

Two minutes passed before Caleb felt safe to move onto the road. They didn't have to go far before he signaled a left turn. He held his breath as a car zipped by him, heading east, but he was able to make the turn before another vehicle, traveling as fast, roared toward Salem.

"Everyone's in a hurry," Annie said as she turned her head to watch the car vanish over abandoned railroad tracks.

"I hope they slow down before they get hurt." Pulling into the asphalt parking area behind the building where ghosts of painted lines were visible, he said, "Here we are."

"Your bakery is going to be here?"

"Ja." He was still amazed he'd been able to buy the building in October.

It had served as a supply depot for the railroad until the mid-1960s. The parking area and the pair of picture windows on the front were perfect for the shop he had in mind. Its wide eaves protected the doors. The building needed painting, but that had to wait for the weather to warm. As a few stray snowflakes wafted toward the ground, he couldn't help imagining how it'd look in May when he planned to open.

"Why a bakery?" she asked.

"My *grossmammi* taught me to bake when I was young, and I enjoyed it." He didn't add he'd been recovering from an extended illness and had been too weak to play outside.

She glanced at him, and he suspected she wanted him to explain further. He didn't.

Walls. Keep up the walls, he reminded himself. Getting close was a one-way ticket to getting hurt again. He wasn't going to do something that *dumm* again.

Not ever.

The wind tore at Annie's coat and shawl when Caleb opened the door on his side and got out. When she reached for her door, he called to her. She had to strain to hear his voice over the wild wind.

"Head inside. Don't wait for me." He grabbed a wool blanket off the floor. "I'll tie up Dusty. I want to put this over him to keep him warm while I give you the nickel tour."

She nodded, but she wasn't sure if he saw the motion because he'd already turned to lash his horse to a hitching rail. The building would provide a windbreak for the horse.

After hurrying through the back door, she paused to cup her hands and blow on them. She wore heavy gloves, but her fingers felt as if they'd already frozen.

It was dusky inside. Large boxes were stacked throughout the cramped space. She wondered what was in them. Not supplies, because the room didn't look ready for use. Paint hung in loose strips between the pair of windows to her left.

She stood on tiptoe to look for writing on the closest box. She halted when she heard a quiet thump.

It came from beyond the crates. She peered around them. A door led into another room.

Was someone there?

Should she get Caleb?

A soft sound, like a gurgle or a gasp, was barely louder than her heartbeat. If someone was in trouble in the other room, she shouldn't hesitate.

God, guide me.

She took a single step toward the other room, keeping her hand on the wall and trying to avoid the big crates. Her eyes widened when she saw a silhouette backlit by a large window. She edged forward, then froze as a board creaked beneath her right foot.

The silhouette whirled. Something struck the floor. A flashlight! It splashed light around the space. A young woman was highlighted before she turned to rush past Annie.

"Wait!" Annie cried.

A *boppli*'s cry echoed through the building.

"Stop!" came a shout from behind Annie.

Caleb!

"There's someone here," she called as she spun, hoping to cut off the woman's escape.

She ran forward at the sound of two bodies hitting each other.

Caleb yelled, "Turn on the lights."

"Lights?"

"Switch…on the wall…by the door." He sounded as if he was struggling with someone.

She flipped the switch and gasped when she saw the person trying to escape from Caleb.

It was a teenage girl, holding a *boppli*. Blonde and cute, the girl had eyes the same dark green as Caleb's. The *boppli* held a bright blue bear close to his cheek and squinted at them in the bright light.

Annie started to ask a question, but Caleb beat her to it when he asked, "Becky Sue? What are you doing *here*?"

Chapter Two

Becky Sue?

Caleb knew this girl and the *boppli*?

Annie wondered why she was surprised. Caleb knew everyone who came to Harmony Creek Hollow. Was this young woman part of a new family joining their settlement? There was one empty farmstead along the twisting road beside the creek.

Annie faltered when she saw the shock on Caleb's face. His green eyes were open so wide she could see white around the irises, and his mouth gaped.

Then she remembered what he'd said after calling the girl by name.

What are you doing here*?*

He wasn't shocked to see Becky Sue. He was shocked she was in his bakery.

What was going on?

As if she'd asked that aloud, Caleb said in a taut tone, "Annie, this is my cousin, Becky Sue Hartz. She and her family have a farm a couple of districts away from where Miriam and I grew up." He closed his mouth, and his jaw worked with strong emotions.

The girl shared Caleb's coloring and his height. Annie wondered how alike they were in other ways.

Stepping forward with a smile, she tried to ignore the thick tension in the air. "I'm Annie Wagler. I should have guessed you were related to Caleb. You look alike."

"Hi, Annie." Becky Sue's eyes kept cutting toward Caleb. Her expression announced she expected to be berated at any second.

Why? For being in the bakery? It wasn't as if she'd broken in. The door had been unlocked. However, even if Becky Sue had jimmied a window and climbed in, her cousin would have forgiven her.

"And who is this cutie?" Annie tapped the nose of the little boy in the girl's arms, and he chuckled in a surprisingly deep tone.

For a moment, Becky Sue lost her hunted look and gave Annie a tentative smile. "This is Joey. He's my son."

Her son? The girl didn't look like much more than a *kind* herself. If Annie had to speculate, she would have guessed Becky Sue was sixteen or seventeen. At the most. The little boy, who had her flaxen hair, appeared to be almost a year old.

Shutting her mouth when she realized it had gaped open as Caleb's was, Annie struggled to keep her smile from falling away. Though it wasn't common, some plain girls got pregnant before marriage as *Englisch* ones did. Or had Becky Sue been a very young bride?

As if she'd cued Caleb, he asked, "Is your husband with you?"

Becky Sue raised her chin in a pose of defiance. A weak one, because her lips trembled, and Annie guessed she was trying to keep from crying.

"No," the girl replied, "because I don't have a husband. Just a son." When Caleb opened his mouth again, she hurried to add, "I'm not a widow, though that would be convenient for everyone, ain't so?"

"Everyone?" He frowned. "Do your parents know where you are?"

"Ja." When he continued to give her a stern look, she relented enough to say, "They know I left home."

"But not where you're going?"

She didn't answer.

"Where *are* you going?" Caleb persisted.

Again the girl was silent, her chin jutting out to show she wasn't going to let him intimidate her. Though the girl was terrified. Her shoulders shook, and her eyes glistened with unshed tears.

Knowing she should keep quiet because the matter was between Caleb and the girl, Annie couldn't halt herself from saying, "I'm sure you and Joey would like something warm to eat. It's cold here, ain't so? Though I was here last winter, I can't get used to it. Caleb, we need to get these two something warm to eat."

Caleb aimed his frown in her direction. She pretended she hadn't seen it. Didn't he understand they wouldn't get any information if the conversation dissolved into the two of them firing recriminations at each other? Once the girl and her *boppli* weren't cold and hungry—and exhausted, because Joey was knuckling his eyes with tiny fists and dark crescents shadowed his *mamm*'s eyes—Becky Sue might be willing to come clean about why she and her son were so far away from home.

But Annie's comments were ignored as Becky Sue

said, "I told you, Caleb. I left home, and I'm—we're not going back."

"And you decided to come to Harmony Creek Hollow?" Annie asked, earning another scowl from Caleb.

"I heard about the new settlement." Though she answered Annie's question, she glared at her cousin. "I didn't know this was the one you were involved with, Caleb. If I had—"

"Well, isn't it a *wunderbaar* coincidence, Becky Sue?" Annie hurried to ask. "And your timing is perfect."

"It is?" Becky Sue seemed overwhelmed by Annie.

Gut! That was what Annie wanted. If the girl stopped thinking about defying Caleb, she might relax enough to reveal a smidgen of the truth; then Annie and Caleb could figure out what was going on.

No! Not Annie and Caleb. She shouldn't use their names together in her thoughts. *She* had to keep *her* focus on helping Caleb see what a *wunderbaar* wife Leanna would make him.

Wishing she could think of a way to bring her twin into the conversation, Annie said, "Your timing is great because Caleb was giving me a tour of his bakery."

"Bakery?" Hope sprang into the girl's voice. "I didn't see any food around here. Do you have some?"

"I've got soup in a thermos in the buggy." Caleb's face eased from its frown. "I meant to eat it for lunch, but I got busy and forgot."

"Wasn't that a blessing?" Annie hoped her laugh didn't sound as forced to them as it did to her.

"It probably won't be hot," Caleb said.

Annie frowned. Didn't he realize his cousin might

be so hungry she wouldn't care what temperature the soup was? "We can heat it up."

He shook his head. "The stove isn't connected. Nothing is yet. The gas company is supposed to have someone come later this week."

Annie made a quick motion with her fingers toward the door. Did he understand that she hoped, when he was gone, Becky Sue would open up to her? Sometimes it was easier to speak to a stranger.

The *boppli* wiggled in Becky Sue's arms and began crying. While the girl's attention was diverted, Annie gestured again to Caleb. He gave her a curt nod, but his frown returned as he headed for the door. If he disliked her idea, why was he going along with it?

Focus, she told herself.

Pasting on a smile, Annie held out her arms to Becky Sue. "Do you want me to hold him while you have something to eat?"

"No, I can do it myself." Her sharp voice suggested she'd made the argument a lot already.

With Becky Sue's parents? Other members of her family? Joey's *daed*? The girl had said she wasn't a widow, but where was the *boppli*'s *daed*?

Wanting to draw Becky Sue out without making the conversation feel like an interrogation, Annie began to talk about the weather again. Her attempts to convince the girl to join in were futile. Becky Sue refused to be lured into talking. Instead she stared at some spot over Annie's head as she bounced her son on her hip in an effort to calm him.

But Annie wasn't going to waste the opportunity. There was one topic any *mamm* would find hard to ignore. "Becky Sue, do you have enough supplies for your *boppli*?"

Her face crumbling as her defiance sifted away, Becky Sue shook her head. "I've only got one clean diaper left for him."

"Do you have bottles, or is he drinking from a cup?"

"I had a bottle." She stared at the floor. "It got lost a couple of days ago."

"My sister-in-law has a little one not too much older than Joey. I'm sure she or someone else will have extra diapers and bottles you can borrow."

Bright tears clung to Becky Sue's lashes, but didn't fall. The girl's strong will astonished Annie. It was also a warning that Becky Sue, unless she decided to cooperate, would continue to avoid answering their questions.

"Gut," the girl replied.

"I know it's none of my business, but are you planning to stay here?"

"You're right. It's not any of your business." A flush rose up Becky Sue's cheeks, and Annie guessed she usually wasn't prickly. In a subdued tone, she added, "I don't know if I'm staying in Harmony Creek Hollow… beyond tonight."

"I'm glad you don't plan to go any farther tonight. It's going to be cold."

"I didn't expect the weather to be so bad."

"None of us did."

Annie watched as the girl began to relax. Becky Sue was willing to talk about trite topics, but the mere hint of any question that delved into why she was in Caleb's bakery made her close up tighter than a miser's wallet.

A few admiring queries about Joey brought a torrent of words from the girl, but they halted when the door opened and Caleb walked in. Annie kept her frustrated sigh to herself as she searched for a chair Caleb said was among the boxes.

Somehow they were going to have to convince the mulish girl to let them help. Becky Sue must be honest with them about what had brought her to northern New York. Annie prayed for inspiration about how to persuade her to trust them.

Not having any ideas on how to solve a problem was a novel sensation.

And it was one she didn't like a bit.

While Becky Sue sat on the floor and began to feed her son small bites of the vegetable soup from the thermos, Caleb watched in silence. The same silence had greeted him when he came into the bakery. He'd heard Annie talking to his cousin, but Becky Sue had cut herself off in the middle of a word the moment she saw him.

Annie edged closer and offered him a kind smile. He was startled at the thought of how comforting it was to have her there. She was focused on what must be done instead of thinking about the implications of his cousin announcing the *boppli* was her son.

But the situation was taking its toll on her, as well. Lines of worry gouged her forehead. She was as upset as he was about his cousin.

"I'm sorry," he murmured.

"For what?" she returned as softly.

"Putting you in the middle of this mess. When I asked you to work for me, I didn't think we'd find my cousin hiding here." He gulped, then forced himself to continue. "Here with a *boppli*."

"You didn't know she was pregnant, ain't so?"

He moved out of the front room. When Becky Sue glanced at them with suspicion, he made sure no emotion was visible on his face. The *boppli* chirped his impatience, and she went back to feeding her son.

Standing where he could watch them, he leaned toward Annie. A whiff of some sweet fragrance, something that offered a tantalizing hint of spring, drifted from her hair. He hadn't thought of Annie Wagler as sweet. She was the forthright one, the one who spoke her mind. But standing close to her, he realized he might have been wrong to dismiss her as all business. She had a feminine side to her.

A very intriguing one.

"Caleb?" she prompted, and he realized he hadn't answered her.

Folding his arms over his coat, he said, "Nobody mentioned anything about Becky Sue having a *kind*."

"But you've got to let her family know she's here. She…"

Annie's voice trailed off, and Caleb looked over his shoulder to see Becky Sue getting to her feet. Annie didn't want his cousin to know they'd been talking about contacting Becky Sue's parents. A wise decision, because making the girl more intractable wouldn't gain them anything.

He realized Annie had guessed the same thing because she strolled into the front room and began asking how Becky Sue and Joey had liked their impromptu picnic.

The girl looked at her coat that was splattered with soup. "He liked it more than you'd guess from the spots on me. I should wash this out before the stains set."

Making sure his tone was conversational, Caleb pointed into the kitchen area and to the right. "The bathroom is through that door."

Becky Sue glanced at her drowsy son and hesitated.

Annie held out her hands. "I'll watch him while you wash up."

"Danki," the girl said as she placed the *boppli* in Annie's arms.

Becky Sue took one step, then paused. She half turned and appraised how Annie cuddled the little boy. Satisfied, she hurried into the bathroom and closed the door.

Annie began to walk the floor to soothe the uneasy *boppli.* He calmed in her arms when she paced from one end of the kitchen to the other. As he stretched out a small hand to touch her face, she said, "This may be the first moment she's had alone since they left home. I can't imagine having to take care of a *boppli* on my own while traveling aimlessly."

"What makes you think she's being aimless?"

"It seems as if she's thought more about running away than running to a specific place."

Caleb nodded at Annie's insightful remark. "We've got to figure out what to do."

"What's to figure out? She has to have a place to stay while you—" She gave a glance at the closed bathroom door. "While you make a few calls."

He was grateful she chose her words with care. If they spooked Becky Sue, she might take off again.

"That's true, but Annie, I live by myself. I can't have her under my roof with nobody else there."

Puzzlement threaded across her brow. "Why not? She's your cousin."

"She's my second cousin."

Comprehension raced through Annie's worried eyes. Marriage between second cousins wasn't uncommon among plain folks. He had two friends who'd made such matches.

"Won't Miriam take them?" she asked, adjusting the *boppli*'s head as it wobbled at the same time he began to snore.

"Under normal circumstances, but she has caught whatever bug has made so many of her scholars sick. When I stopped by earlier today, the whole family were barely able to get on their feet. She won't want to pass along the germs."

"Then there's only one solution."

"What's that?"

"She can stay at our house."

To say he was shocked would have been an understatement. "But they're not your problem."

She gave him a frown he guessed had daunted many others. He squared his shoulders before she realized how successful her expression nearly had been.

"Caleb, Becky Sue and Joey aren't a problem. Becky Sue is a girl *with* a problem. Not that this little one should be called a problem, either." Her face softened when she gazed at the sleeping *boppli* in her arms and rocked him.

He almost gasped, as he had when he recognized his cousin among the boxes in the bakery's kitchen. The unguarded warmth on Annie's face offered a view of her he'd never seen before. He wondered how many had, because she hid this gentle softness behind a quick wit and sharp tongue. He was discovering many aspects of her today. He couldn't help being curious about what else she kept concealed.

"We've got plenty of room in our house," she went on, her voice rising and falling with the motion of her arms as she rocked the *kind*. "There will always be someone there to help Becky Sue."

He couldn't argue. The twins' younger sister, Juanita, was in her final year of school. In addition, Annie's *grossmammi* and younger brother lived with them.

At that thought, he said, "You've already got your hands full."

"True, so we won't notice another couple of people in our house. Let us help you, Caleb. You've worked hard building our community, and doing this will give our family a chance to repay you."

Guilt suffused him, but he couldn't think of another solution. It seemed Becky Sue had already decided she could trust Annie. Now he must show he trusted her, too.

The bathroom door opened and Becky Sue emerged. When Annie asked her to stay with the Wagler family, she made the invitation sound spontaneous.

Caleb held his breath until his cousin said, *"Danki."*

"Get your things," he replied. "I turned the heater on in the buggy when I got the thermos. It's as warm in there as it's going to be, so bundle up. I'll stop by later and check on you."

"You aren't coming with us?" Becky Sue asked suspiciously.

"No. I've got work to do." Turning to Annie, he said with the best smile he could manage, "You taking them tonight will let me keep my work on schedule."

"Gut," Annie replied, as if the timetable for the bakery was the most important thing on their minds.

As soon as Becky Sue went into the front room, Caleb lowered his voice. "*Danki* for taking her home with you. Now I'll have the chance to contact her family."

"Do they have access to a phone?"

"I'm pretty sure they do. If not, I can try calling the store that's not far from where they live. The *Englisch* owner will deliver emergency messages." He couldn't keep from arching his brows. "I don't know what would constitute more of an emergency than a missing *kind* and *kins-kind*."

"You know the number?"

"The phone here at the bakery is for dealing with vendors, but I've let a couple of our neighbors use it, and at least one of them mentioned calling the store. The number should be stored in the phone's list of outgoing calls."

Becky Sue returned with a pair of torn and dirty grocery bags in one hand. The girl carried a bright blue and yellow blanket in the other. Stains on it suggested she and her *boppli* had slept rough since leaving their home.

Joey woke as Annie was wrapping the blanket around him. He took one look at Caleb and began to cry at a volume Caleb hadn't imagined a little boy could make.

As Annie cooed to console him, she handed him to his *mamm*. She finished winding the blanket around him at the same time as she herded Becky Sue out of the bakery.

Caleb went to a window and watched them leave in his buggy. He went to the phone he kept on top of the rickety cabinet that must be as old as the building. He'd planned to start tearing the cupboard out after giving Annie a tour of the bakery. He wondered when he'd have time to finish.

Soon, he told himself. He'd set a date at the beginning of May to open the bakery. He'd already purchased ads in the local newspaper and the swap magazine delivered to every household in the area because his customers from the farmer's market had been so insistent he inform them as soon as the bakery opened its doors.

Picking up the phone, he frowned when he began clicking through the list of outgoing calls. Someone had made a call about ten minutes before he and Annie had arrived. He had no doubt it was Becky Sue.

The number wasn't a Lancaster County one. It had a different area code, one he didn't recognize. He wasn't sure where 319 was, but he'd ask someone at the fire department where he was a volunteer firefighter to look it up for him.

But that had to wait. For now…

He found the number for the small store and punched it in. This wouldn't be an easy call.

Chapter Three

As Annie had expected, her arrival with Becky Sue and the *boppli* in tow threw the Wagler house into an uproar. The moment they walked in, her two sisters stopped their preparations for supper and came over to greet their unexpected guests. The family's new puppy, Penny, who was a hound and Irish setter mix Annie's younger brother had brought home the previous week, barked and bounced as if she had springs for legs.

Annie's efforts to catch Penny were worthless. The copper-colored pup was too eager to greet the newcomers to listen. Little Joey seemed as excited as the puppy. Becky Sue had to wrap him in both arms to keep him from escaping.

Pulling off her coat, Annie tossed it over a nearby chair. She finally was able to grab Penny by the ruff. The puppy wore a mournful expression when Annie shut her in the laundry room. She hoped Penny would calm down at the sight of her dish filled with kibble.

Annie returned to the kitchen and looked around. A bolt of concern riveted her. *Grossmammi* Inez wasn't in the rocking chair by the living room door. Her *gross-*

mammi had lived with them for a year after Annie's *daed* died from a long illness. When Annie's *mamm* married her late husband's cousin and had two more *kinder*, Annie had used any excuse to visit her *grossmammi.*

The elderly woman had taken them in a second time after *Mamm* and her second husband, a hardworking man who'd been a loving *daed* to his stepchildren, were killed in a bus accident when Kenny was a toddler. Though she couldn't do as much as she once had, *Grossmammi* Inez supervised the kitchen she considered her domain.

"She's resting," Leanna said before she shot a smile at Becky Sue and introduced herself.

Annie nodded, glad her twin knew what was on her mind. However, her uneasiness didn't ebb. Her *grossmammi* sometimes took a nap, but Annie couldn't recall her ever staying in bed while meal preparations were underway.

Her attention was drawn to her guests when Becky Sue asked, "You are twins, ain't so?" The teenager stared, wide-eyed at Leanna before facing Annie. "You look exactly alike."

Leanna said with a faint smile, "I'm a quarter inch taller."

"Really?"

Leanna lifted her right foot. "Only when I'm wearing these sneakers."

Everyone, including Becky Sue, laughed, and Annie wanted to hug her twin for putting the girl at ease.

"I've never met girl twins before," Becky Sue said. "There were two pairs of boy twins in my school, but no girls."

"No?" Annie laughed again. "Well, now you have."

Before Becky Sue could reply, Annie's younger sister, Juanita, edged around Leanna. She was a gangly fourteen-year-old who was already three inches taller than the twins and still growing, though Annie doubted she'd ever challenge Becky Sue's height. Juanita's light brown hair was so tightly curled it popped out around her *kapp* in hundreds of tiny coils. It was the bane of Juanita's existence, and nothing she'd tried had straightened it enough to keep the strands in place.

"Can I hold him?" Juanita held out her arms to the *boppli*.

Annie smiled at her younger sister. Juanita wavered between being a *kind* herself and becoming a young woman. It was shocking to realize Becky Sue couldn't have been much older than Juanita when she became pregnant. Annie's sister hadn't begun to attend youth events yet, preferring to spend time with girls her own age. They seemed more interested in besting the boys at sports than flirting.

"This is my sister Juanita," she explained to Becky Sue. "We've got two brothers, as well. Lyndon is married and lives next door, and Kenny, who's twelve, should be out in the barn milking with him. You'll meet him at supper."

Juanita cuddled Joey, who reached up to touch her face as he had Annie's. Becky Sue took off her coat and hung it up by the door as she scanned the large kitchen with cabinets along one wall and the refrigerator and stove on another.

Standing by the large table in the center, Annie smiled at her younger sister who loved all young things. She delighted in taking care of the farm's animals, other than Leanna's goats and the dairy cows. She tended to the chickens, ducks and geese as well as the pigs and two sheep.

When Joey began fussing, Annie urged her sisters to return to making supper while she took Becky Sue upstairs and got her and the *boppli* settled. The extra bed was in Annie's room, but if Becky Sue was bothered by the arrangement, she didn't mention it. Annie cleared out the deepest drawer in her dresser and folded a quilt in it. Tucking a sheet around the quilt, she added a small blanket on top to make a bed for Joey. She urged her guests to rest while she went to help her sisters finish supper.

Annie asked Juanita to run next door to ask their sister-in-law if they could borrow some diapers and a couple of bottles for the *boppli*. Her younger sister was always happy for any excuse to visit her nephews and nieces.

Leanna didn't pause chopping vegetables for the stew simmering on the gas stove. Not that her twin would do any actual cooking. Juanita was already a more competent cook.

Hanging up the coat she'd draped over the kitchen chair, Annie went to the stove and checked the beef stew. She halted, her fingers inches from the spoon, as she wondered if Caleb would be joining them for supper. He'd said something about coming over after he called Becky Sue's parents.

"We need to set extra plates on the table," Annie said as she stirred the stew so it didn't stick.

"More than one?" Leanna looked up from the trio of carrots she had left to chop.

"Caleb said he'd stop over." Annie dropped her voice

to a whisper to explain why he'd remained behind at the bakery. "It'll be a *gut* opportunity for us to get to know him better."

Her twin set down the knife and walked away from the counter. Taking the broom from its corner, she began to sweep the kitchen floor. "Why were you at the bakery today?"

"Caleb wants an assistant to help with getting it ready and to wait on customers when it opens. He asked me, though he thought he was asking you." She told Leanna about the conversation by the goats' pen. "If you'd like to take the job instead, I'm sure he'd agree."

Leanna stopped sweeping. "I've already got a job."

That was true. Leanna cleaned for several *Englisch* neighbors. She could have a house sparkling in less time than it took Annie to do a load of wash.

"This would be different." Her answer sounded lame even to Annie, but somehow she had to convince her sister to be honest about her feelings for Caleb.

Leanna was generous and kind and, other than her inability to cook and bake, something that shouldn't be as important to a man who owned a bakery, would make Caleb a *wunderbaar* wife. It was a fabulous plan, even if it broke Annie's own heart.

Frustration battered her. Why couldn't those two see what was obvious to Annie? Leanna and Caleb could make each other happy as husband and wife. Of that, she was certain.

Because you believe you *would be happy with him as his wife.*

Annie wished her conscience would remain silent. It was true she'd imagined walking out with Caleb before she noticed how her sister reacted each time he was near.

God, make me Your instrument in bringing happiness to Leanna, she prayed as she had so many times since her sister's heart was broken.

"It doesn't matter," Leanna said, "whether the job is different or not. I wouldn't have time to work for Caleb. This morning, I agreed to clean Mrs. Duchamps's house twice a week."

Annie recognized the name of one of the few *Englischers* who lived along the meandering creek. Mrs. Duchamps had worked at the bank in Salem most of her adult life as well taking care of her late husband during the years when he was ill. Having no *kinder* of her own, it was no surprise Mrs. Duchamps had hired Leanna to help.

"I didn't know you were looking for more houses to clean."

Leanna smiled. "I enjoy the work, so why not? And we could use the money. Kenny is growing so fast it seems as if he needs new shoes every other month. This works out for the best because I wouldn't want to work at Caleb's bakery." She began sweeping again. "Don't you think it's odd he wants to start a bakery at the same time he's trying to keep his farm going?"

"Not really." Annie recalled the light beaming from his eyes when he spoke about his plans for the bakery. It was a chance to make his dream a reality.

"Then it's a *gut* thing he asked you instead of me." Leanna shuddered. "I don't know what I'd say to his customers, and I'd get so nervous I'd end up dropping a tray of cookies."

"You navigate among your goats without stumbling. Even when you're milking them."

Leanna laughed. "Having them crowd around me hides a lot of my clumsiness. Besides, I'm sure you're going to have *wunderbaar* ideas to help Caleb."

"Maybe. Maybe not." Annie began to chop the rest of the carrots.

"You never used to hesitate sharing your ideas, Annie. I wish I had half of the ones you have."

"Ideas come when they come."

Ideas did always pop into her head. She used to speak them without hesitation, but that was before she'd started walking out with Rolan Plank three years ago. They hadn't lasted long as a couple. After a month, he'd started to scold her for speaking up. He chided her for what he'd called her silly ideas. Yet, after he'd dumped her, he'd taken one of her so-called silly ideas and let everyone think it was his own.

"Either way," Leanna said, "I'm glad you're working for Caleb instead of me."

"But you could have had a chance to get to know him better."

"True, but I'm sure you'll share many stories about your time with him." Leanna paused for a long moment, then added, "I didn't think we'd still be talking about jobs now. I assumed I'd be a wife and *mamm*, but that hasn't happened."

"It will when—"

"Don't tell me it's God's will whether I marry or not." Her twin kept moving, each motion sure and calm in comparison with her voice. "I've heard that too many times."

Annie paid no attention to her sister's words. Only to

her heartbroken tone, and Annie's heart broke, as well. Her sister had fallen hard for Gabriel Miller before they moved from Lancaster County, but Gabriel had wed someone else. In retrospect, Annie wasn't sure he'd been aware of Leanna's feelings. As far as Annie knew, her sister hadn't told him. Instead, she'd decided to let him pursue her as the heroes did the heroines in the romance novels Leanna loved to read.

In the months since they'd arrived at the settlement in Harmony Creek Hollow, her sister had begun to emerge from her self-imposed isolation. Being a member of the Harmony Creek Spinsters' Club with two of their friends had helped. Now their friends Miriam and Sarah were married. In fact, there had been three weddings at the end of the year, and while Leanna was thrilled for her friends, each ceremony had been a reminder of what she wanted and didn't have: a husband and a family of her own.

Annie scooped up the chopped carrots and dropped them into the stew. When Caleb had offered her the job—even if it'd appeared to be a mistake—God had opened a door for her to help her sister. She ignored the familiar twinge in her own heart as she tried to convince herself that persuading Caleb to walk out with her twin sister would be the best idea she'd ever had.

How was it possible the evening was growing colder by the second? Each breath Caleb took seemed to be more glacial than the one before. He hadn't thought it could get any more bitter, but with the sun setting, the very air felt as if it'd turned to ice. He guessed by the time he'd left the bakery, gotten home and milked his cows, the mercury must have dropped to ten degrees below zero. It would be worse by the time he got up in the morning. The idea of heading into his comfortable house and calling it a day had been tempting, but he couldn't cede his responsibility for his cousin and her *kind* to Annie. He'd told her he'd stop by, and he couldn't renege on the promise.

As he led Dusty toward the Waglers' barn so the horse could get out of the cold, Caleb glanced at the goats' pen. It was empty, and he guessed the goats were huddling inside their shed.

Smart goats. He smiled at the two words he'd never thought he would put together.

Caleb's shoulders ached by the time he walked to the house. Trying to halt the shivers rippling over him was foolish, because he couldn't relax against the cold. His body refused to keep from trying to keep the polar wind at bay.

He climbed up onto the porch and rapped on the door. The faint call from inside was all the invitation he needed to open it.

Taking one step inside the mudroom connecting the kitchen to the porch, he was almost bowled over by a reddish-brown ball of fur. A sharp command from the table didn't stop the excited puppy from welcoming him.

Kenny rushed into the mudroom to collect the dog. Caleb smiled his thanks to the dark-haired boy before shrugging off his coat. Watching Kenny try to get the puppy to behave with little success, Caleb wondered if the boy's shoulders grew broader every day. Kenny wasn't going to be tall, but he was going to be a sturdy adult. Hard work in the barn was giving him the strength of a man twice his age.

Caleb set his coat, scarf, gloves and hat on a chair

by the door because the pegs were filled. He turned to walk into the kitchen and then stopped as he took in the sight of the families gathered around the table. Two families. The Waglers—Annie and her twin as well as her *grossmammi*, sister and younger brother, who was sliding into his chair, holding onto the puppy—and two members of the Hartz family: his cousin and her son.

Yet they could have been a single family. No one acted disconcerted. One twin held Joey on her lap and offered him bites of her food while his cousin sat on the opposite side of the table between a girl close to her age and the other twin.

But which twin was which? He was embarrassed that he wasn't sure.

His discomfort was overtaken by distress. He hadn't been able to reach Becky Sue's parents. He'd waited by the phone at the bakery for an hour, hoping for a call back. He'd left after that because his dairy herd got uncomfortable when he delayed the milking.

"*Komm* in…and join us," Inez said, motioning to him.

The elderly woman was shorter than the twins, and though her hair was gray and thinning, she had the same blue-green eyes. It was more than a physical resemblance, because she said what she thought, exactly as Annie did.

"*Komm*…in, Caleb," Inez urged again when he didn't move. She paused often as if having to catch her breath. "Sit…so we…can thank God…for our food…before… everything…is cold."

He entered the kitchen, which smelled of beef gravy and freshly baked bread. When his stomach rumbled, a reminder he'd skipped lunch, he was glad he was far enough away from the table so nobody would hear it. "You could have eaten without me."

"See?" piped up Kenny. "I told you he'd be okay with it."

"But… I wasn't." Inez's tone brooked no argument, and the boy didn't give her any as he bent to soothe the puppy who was lunging to escape so it could greet Caleb as he neared the table. "Hurry. Join…us before hunger… makes Kenny forget…his manners again."

When the twin holding Joey—Caleb was almost certain she was Annie—flashed him a quick smile, he dampened his own. He admired how Inez spoke her mind. Not that she ever was cruel or critical of anyone, though she denounced what she saw as absurd ideas. She, as one of his fellow firefighters was fond of saying, called it as she saw it.

The only empty chair was at the end of the table. He sat there and nodded when Inez asked him to lead grace. He was the oldest man present, and it was his duty. As he bowed his head, his thoughts refused to focus on his gratitude for God guiding his young cousin to the bakery where she could be found. He was too aware of both twins sitting at the table.

If he mistook one for the other…

Annie had given him an easy way to avoid admitting he hadn't realized which twin he was asking to work for him, but he couldn't depend on that happening again.

He cleared his throat to signal the end of grace. As he raised his head, he was startled by an abrupt yearning he hadn't expected. A yearning for a life where he could sit with a family of his own at day's end. Several of his friends had married in November and December and stepped into the next phase of their lives. He was moving forward as well, but not in the same direction. Was he missing his chance to have a family?

There wasn't time for such thoughts. Between the farm and the bakery, he had too much work to do every day. The responsibilities of a family would require more of his nonexistent time. He'd made his choice, and he shouldn't second-guess himself.

Caleb took the bowl of fragrant stew. He spooned some onto his plate, then more when urged by Inez, who told him in her no-nonsense voice not to worry if he emptied the bowl because there was extra on the stove. When he sampled it, he was glad he'd listened to the old woman.

He focused on eating as conversation went on around him. He looked up when Inez spoke.

"Leanna…pass the basket…of rolls…to Caleb." Inez gave him a wink as she spoke with her usual interruptions. Seeing how the twins glanced at her, he wondered what her pauses to take a breath meant. "I've…never met a…man who doesn't…have room for…another roll…or two."

"Especially with apple butter," he replied as he waited to see which twin did as her *grossmammi* had asked. When it wasn't the one holding Joey, he was relieved. He'd guessed Annie was the twin bouncing the little boy on her knee and keeping Joey entertained with pieces of soft carrot she'd fished out of her stew. He watched, amazed at how she kept the *kind* fed while she ate her own supper. He was beginning to wonder if Annie was *gut* at everything she did. She'd handled the touchy situation with Becky Sue with a skill he didn't possess.

"I'm not as out of practice as I thought," Annie said

with a laugh. Was she trying to put him at ease for staring? That she might be able to discern his thoughts was disquieting. "I used to feed Kenny this way when he was little."

Kenny grumbled something, and Caleb swallowed his chuckle. No boy on the verge of becoming a teenager wanted to be reminded about such things.

As the meal went on and Caleb had another generous serving of the delicious stew, laughter came from the Waglers. But Becky Sue was reticent, and every movement she made displayed exhaustion. He wondered when—and where—she'd last slept.

A quick prayer of gratitude for their food, their families and for shelter from the cold night ended the meal. Leanna offered to help Becky Sue upstairs so she could rest, and Inez took the *boppli* into the living room to rock him until he became sleepy. Kenny wandered off somewhere with the puppy he called Penny.

Annie began to clear the table, carrying the dishes to the white farmhouse sink. "Did you get in touch with Becky Sue's parents?"

"No answer yet."

"As soon as they get the message, they'll call. I can't imagine how happy they'll be to discover their daughter and *kins-kind* are safe with you."

"With you, actually."

"We're happy to help." When he picked up his dishes, she said, "You don't have to clear the table. I know you've had a long day."

"No longer than yours."

"But I didn't have to milk." She laughed. "Lyndon, Kenny and Leanna milk every day, and Juanita will help sometimes. I always try to find somewhere else to be."

"Why? There's something *wunderbaar* about being in a warm barn and spending time with animals willing to share their bounty with us." He set the dishes by the sink. "For me, it's one of the clearest symbols of God's gifts to us."

She turned on the water and squirted dish detergent into the sink. "That's a much nicer way of looking at milking."

"But not your way?"

"Definitely not." She chuckled as she reached for the dishrag.

"You may have your mind changed one of these days."

"Don't hold your breath."

He smiled. Trust Annie Wagler not to withhold her opinion! It was one of the reasons his sister liked her, and working together at the bakery was going to be interesting. At least he wouldn't have to try to guess what she was thinking.

"So you prefer spending time with a *boppli* who spits up on you rather than a nice, clean cow who gives you milk?"

"Spits up?" She glanced at the spots of orange on her black apron. "I didn't notice. Oh, well. It'll wash out." She laughed. "Joey should be glad he wanted to sit on my lap rather than Leanna's."

"Why?" He was curious how the little boy had figured out which twin was which. And a bit envious of the *kind*'s intuitive ability.

"Leanna prefers *boppli* goats to *boppli* humans because she spent most of her teen years babysitting for an *Englisch* family who had a ton of rules about their *kinder*. They insisted she carry the *boppli* in some sort of contraption that wrapped around her shoulders.

Half the time when she came home, she was covered with formula because they believed she should feed the *boppli* in the getup."

"That's enough to put anyone off from *kinder*."

Annie flinched, surprising him before she went to the table to collect more dishes. "She won't feel that way about her own *bopplin*. She'll be a *wunderbaar mamm*, I know."

"But you'll never like milking?"

"Never!" She carried the other dishes to the sink.

"Don't you know you should never say never?"

"That sounds like a challenge."

"It might be."

"It's one you're guaranteed to lose. Cows and I agree we're better off having as little to do with each as possible."

"You're going to make me prove that you're wrong."

"About what?" asked Inez as she came into the kitchen. She set Joey on the floor and pressed one hand to her chest. An odd wheezing sound came from her, and she sat in the closest chair.

Annie rushed to her side. "Are you okay, *Grossmammi*?"

"I guess I'm not as young as I used to be." She glanced at the *boppli,* who dropped to his belly. "Chasing a young one is a task for someone with fewer years on her than me. So, what you are going to prove our Annie wrong about, Caleb?"

"That milking is a pleasant chore," he replied, though he wondered how Inez had failed so fast.

Beside her chair, Annie looked worried, but she kept her voice light. "*That* is something he'll never prove to me. *Grossmammi*, I can finish up if you want to go to bed."

He thought Inez would protest it was too early, but she didn't. Coming to her feet, she said, "A *gut* idea. These old bones need extra rest to keep up with a *boppli*." Before he could say he'd make other arrangements for Becky Sue, she added, "Caleb, we're glad to have your cousin and her *kind* stay with us." She wagged a gnarled finger at him. "Such things should go unsaid among neighbors, ain't so?"

Again, as he bid Inez a *gut nacht*, he was discomfited at how the Wagler women seemed to gauge his thoughts.

At the very moment Inez closed the door to her bedroom beyond the kitchen, Joey began to crawl toward them on his belly. Caleb bent to pick up the little fellow, but froze when Joey let out a shriek. The *boppli* clenched his fists close to his sides as his face became a vivid red.

"What's wrong?" Caleb asked as he reached again for the *kind*.

With a screech that rang in Caleb's ears, Joey cringed away.

Annie scooped up the *boppli* and held him close as she murmured. Joey's heart-rending screams dissolved into soft, gulping sobs as he buried his face in her neck. She patted his back and made soothing sounds into his hair. When the *boppli* softened against her, she looked over his head toward Caleb.

Sympathy battled with dismay in her expressive eyes. Caleb had never guessed a mere look could convey such intense emotion. Or maybe it was as simple as the fact he felt sorry for the toddler, too.

Becky Sue burst into the kitchen, wearing a borrowed robe over a nightgown too short for her. Her hair was half braided and her *kapp* was missing. "What's wrong with Joey?"

"I think he's overtired," Annie said. "*Bopplin* get strange notions in their heads when they're Joey's age. Some don't like men. Others fear dogs or cats or tiny bugs."

"Do you know why he's scared of men?" Caleb didn't want to admit how relieved he was Joey's antipathy wasn't aimed solely at him, because he'd always gotten along well with *kinder.*

Becky Sue shrugged. Or she tried to, but her shoulders must have been as stiff as his had been outside in the cold, because they curtailed the motion. Instead of answering him further, she hefted her son and walked away.

Caleb watched her climb the stairs at the front of the house and vanish along with the *boppli.* Her lack of answer told him plenty. She was hiding even more than he'd guessed.

Don't miss
The Amish Bachelor's Baby *by Jo Ann Brown,*
available March 2019 wherever
Love Inspired® books and ebooks are sold.
www.Harlequin.com

Finally following his dreams of opening a bakery, Caleb Hartz hires Annie Wagler as his assistant. But they both get more than they bargain for when his runaway teenage cousin and her infant son arrive. Can they work together to care for mother and child—without falling in love?

Read on for a sneak preview of The Amish Bachelor's Baby *by Jo Ann Brown, available February 2019 from Love Inspired!*

"I wanted to talk to you about a project I'm getting started on. I'm opening a bakery."

"You are?" Annie couldn't keep the surprise out of her voice.

"*Ja,*" Caleb said. "I stopped by to see if you'd be interested in working for me."

"You want to hire me? To work in your bakery?"

"I've had some success selling bread and baked goods at the farmers' market in Salem. Having a shop will allow me to sell year-round, but I can't be there every day and do my work at the farm. My sister Miriam told me you'd do a *gut* job for me."

"It sounds intriguing," Annie said. "What would you expect me to do?"

"Tend the shop and handle customers. There would be some light cleaning. I may need you to help with baking sometimes."

"*Ja*, I'd be interested in the job."

"Then it's yours. If you've got time now, I'll give you a tour of the bakery, and we can talk more about what I'd need you to do."

"Gut." The wind buffeted her, almost knocking her from her feet.

She mumbled that she needed to let her twin, Leanna, know where she was going. He wrapped his arms around himself as another blast of wind struck them.

"Hurry…anna…" The wind swallowed the rest of his words as she rushed toward the house.

She halted midstep.

Anna?

Had Caleb thought he was talking to her twin? She'd clear everything up on their way to the bakery. She wanted the job. It was an answer to so many prayers, for God to let her find a way to help her sister be happy again, happy as Leanna had been before the man she loved married someone else without telling her.

Leanna was attracted to Caleb, and he'd be a fine match for her. Outgoing where her twin was quiet. A well-respected, handsome man whose *gut* looks would be the perfect foil for her twin's. But Leanna would be too shy to let Caleb know she was interested in him. That was where Annie could help.

As she was rushing to the house, she reminded herself of one vital thing. She must be careful not to let her own attraction to Caleb grow while they worked together.

That might be the hardest part of the job.

LIEXP0219

SPECIAL EXCERPT FROM

When criminal lawyer Tyler Everson witnesses a murder, he becomes the killer's next target—along with his estranged wife, Annabelle, and their daughter. Now they need to enter witness protection in Amish country.

Read on for a sneak preview of
Amish Haven *by Dana R. Lynn,*
the exciting conclusion of the Amish Witness Protection miniseries, available March 2019 from
Love Inspired Suspense!

Annie was cleaning up the dishes when the phone rang. She didn't recognize the number.

"Hello?"

"Annie, it's me."

Tyler.

Her estranged husband. The man she hadn't seen in two years.

"Annie? You there?"

She shook her head. "Yes, I'm here. It's been a frazzling day, Tyler. What do you want?"

A pause. "Something's happened last night, Annie. I can't tell you everything, but the US Marshals are involved. I'm being put into witness protection."

"Witness protection? Tyler, people in those programs have to completely disappear."

In her mind, she heard Bethany ask when she would see her daddy again.

"I know. It won't be forever. At least I hope it won't. I need to testify against someone. Maybe after that, I can go back to being me."

A sudden thought occurred to her. "Tyler, the reason you're going into witness protection… Would it affect me at all?"

"What do you mean?"

"Someone was following me today."

"Someone's following you?" Tyler exclaimed, horrified.

"You never answered. Could the man following me be related to what happened to you?"

"I don't know. Annie, I will call you back." He disconnected the call and went down the hall.

Marshal Mast was sitting at a laptop in an office at the back of the house. He glanced up from the screen as Tyler entered. "Something on your mind, Tyler?"

"I called my wife to tell her I was going into witness protection. She said she and my daughter were being followed today."

At this information, Jonathan Mast jumped to his feet. "Karl!"

Feet pounded in the hallway. Marshal Karl Adams entered the room at a brisk pace. "Jonathan? Did you need me?"

"Yes, I need you to make a trip for me. What's the address, Tyler?"

Tyler recited the address. Would Karl and Stacy get there in time? How he wished he could go with him…

Don't miss
Amish Haven *by Dana R. Lynn,*
available March 2019 wherever
Love Inspired® Suspense books and ebooks are sold.

www.LoveInspired.com

LISEXP0219